In the shadow of socitey

A book of Jesper Persson

Earlier edition 2008

"From Smith to criminal and the way back"

2012

"The mistake of operation government" Part 1

2013

"The mistake of operation government" Part 2

My motto: Trust is good – Control is better

A special thanks to mentioned below!

To my kids Tobias and Alexander which gave me the power to finish this book.

I will also thanks all the people who bought my books. For me, it´s a proof that our Community are in imbalance.

I will give a special thanks to P.U.D, who helped me write all the notepads I wrote and dictated to a document on the computer, so I could send the document to the press.
Because of the Stroke I`ve had, I don`t have fine motorics to write so fast anymore. You`re worth gold.

FSC
www.fsc.org
MIX
Papper från
ansvarsfulla källor
Paper from
responsible sources
FSC® C105338

Prologue

In this book, you will, as a reader, know how it really are, to sit in the slammer, and how it`s affected me as a person. I`ve been by the State international called for, and you will see which the consequences been after my decisions. You will know how it is to be called for international, and how I wanted a life under the radar in this community. It can be really heavy to write your memoirs when you over and over again have to go through all the shit I`ve done. You will follow when I´ve got the heart attack, and after that Stroke, which made me wan on the left side, two month after my heartattack, and how I`ve been fighting for my come back to a normal life. As a reader you even can see, how the swedish prisons influenced the person who`s inmate. It`s a really hard reality you as a reader have in the front of you, and I`m most certainly it is gonna influenced you, positive or negative. You will follow me into correctional treatment, where I have served mine sentence imprisonment for a long time. You will also got to know all the frustrated feelings I had during this time. You will learn about the difference between the average Swede as an inmate in the hands of the correctional treatment, and you`re deprived of liberty. You will see with your own eyes how the correctional treatment manipulated mine appeal by not sending my plaint too ombudsmannen. Like I always use to say stop reading now, if you`re a sensitive person which influence by negative stuff. I think that you as a reader, have to know the incredible important truth, how the community works. After that, you self can form an opinion, about the living in a manipulated community.
Much pleasure!

Chapter: 1 The heartattack

I had a feeling, there was some hassle with my pump, (heart), and I didn`t think so much about it. I`ve lift some boxes during the day, and I thought that I have strayed beyond after all the heft. I want to complete what I was doing during the day, and i did. When I was to interfere in the evening, I felt that it hurts in mine scapula and it starts to emit in my left arm. It was a strange feeling when it consisted to emit hurts in my left arm. For me, it`s been a sleepless night. The pain were very high, so I couldn`t sleep. In the early hours in the morning, I was very tired, and I haven`t sleep because of the pain. My friends want me to, go to hospital to check the heart, and I did. The nurse takes me to emergencyroom, there was monitors all over the room. All this monitors, and a nurse who running arounds me, it stressed me up. I would like to walk away from the room. The Nurse come to my bunk, and wanted to know my bloodpressure, -Yes, you can, I answer. She put a cuff on my right arm and listen with an stethoscope. My bloodpressure was very high, 200/105, and the nurse told me it wasn`t good, and she asked me if I was stressed?

- How, will you believe? I asked here.

– Your bloodpressure is very high, she say, and she was worried for my bloodpressure, and she`s gonna talk to the doctor. She`s taking me to lab for a bloodtest soon as posible. There are some marker, and they want to see if they were increased. The name of the marker is Troponin, and it is a biochemical marker which being released when you have a harm in the muscle of your heart.

It`s time to put on the ECG on me, so the doctor will have lots of information about my heart, and if there were other damages in my heart.

Electrokardiographi, or ECG like we use to say, is a method to illustrate the activity of the heart. The nurse want me to be calm while they took my ECG. So I was. I thought it was really annoying with all the thoughts I have. It was a lot of pain that remind me, and create all the thoughts which absolutely affliction me. I know that while they took my ECG, I was at the right place if anything will happen, and I keep myself to that thought.

I lay there and look at all the monitors, and it was a frightening feeling. The nurse said – it`s ready. Now she`s gonna give it to the doctor, so he could se if I had any heartattack, and if the markers had gained according the bloodtest I`ve taken. Now I`m broken to an ordinary room, while I been waiting for the doctor to come in. There wasn`t so much stuff as, it was in the emergency room. There was not any monitors at all. The room was much minor. I had the worry, and a frustration that really concerned me. I was scared that my heart would stop, or something else would happend. My thoughts went to all the check I`ve been taken, and what they`re gonna show. Did I had an heartattack, or not. Were my marker increased? The questions directly didn`t clear with their absence. The doctor came and told me, that I`ve had an heartattack at night, and my marker were absence, and the doctor is going to impose me at the hospital. A nurse came and put something down on my legs, which will start my heart if it suddenly stop in the elevator, when I´m going up to the ward. According the nurse they have to do that, so the patient will be safe during the trip in the elevator. Well up on the ward, the doctor want to bring down mine blood-pressure, it was 200/105, and he`s gonna put in some medication to fix my bloodpressure.

The responsible male nurse understood that I´m not like to take medicine, and I was really challenge about the conversant medicin. The malenurse got to insurance that it was good medicin, like the doctor put in, and it wasn`t dangerous at all, this word could not persuade me, I had an idea just to take half the dose, and se how I feel. Now in hindsight, it feels really imbecilic, not to trust your doctors ordination, to take that medicine he foresaw. It got to me that the medications wasn`t good for me, at least not the hole dosage. In hindsight, I can see that I play with my own life. Like I know better than my own doctor. As you read, I have my ideas. Well, the doctor has been and talked with me. He want to se the pressure in the morning, and if it wasn`t good he wanted to do a baloonexplosion tomorrow.

Now it`s only the night to get through. The night started in a good and calm way. I have this nabour, and it was just a drape between us, which symbolize a wall, so it was very perceptively. In the evening I look at the television, and when I´m doing that, suddenly the busterbugger start to snore. It´s just like he has to sync my remote control, even when I need to screw up, he snored higher and higher. I´ve been tired for less, I blow up the tv and put a pillow on my ear so I could sleep. It could been worse, the old man could start to rub teeth. In the morning when I went past him, I saw that he could not begin to rub teeth, because his teeth were in a glass of water on the bedside table.

It´s morning and time for the baloonexplosion. The doctor said that the operation is during the day. I´m gonna take a shower according the doctor, and washed myself with an especially faunding, and this faunding were antimicrobial, and I´m gonna do it before the operation.
I stood in the shower and washed myself with the yellow antimicrobial faunding. When I´m ready I went to my room, and after a while I track down for operation.

Chapter 2: The operation

The nurses who drove me down for operation, stayed in the corridor, so I had to wait for my turn for operation. There were many people, for operation, so I got to be nice and wait for my turn. At least it`s my turn. When I come into the operationroom, there were two nurses and they took care of me. One of the nurses start to wash my leg, and it`s including my balls. I thought this was annoying. She washed me with some founding that burned pretty well. I see soon that I have lucky to survive after this heartattack.

The feeling that comes over me, was frightening, what if my heart stopped? They want to take a bloodpressure, and it was absolutely high. The operationdoctor called the doctor on the ward, and told him about my blood pressure. The doctors agree that I´m not having the serguy because there wasn`t any profit to operate right now. The nurses drive me back to my room, because it`s not gonna be any operation. The fact is that I have this bloodpressure the doctors dont want me to have. When I´m back on the ward, I began to thought about what I actually did. Would I play with my own life or listen to what the doctor said. It`s easy to see that I made my own body this disservice. I live a life which are not good for my body anymore.
I knew I lived a decent hard life and the consequence is this heartattack. It`s easy to make a promise to youself that you gonna be a better person. The boring thing is, that you almost being negative again, and live a life which is negative. I should have learn myself after all the shit, it was at least something I was hoping.

The doctor want me to stay at the hospital. Would this night be sign in frustration? I could only hope that the person, not gonna snore. By the round, my ordinary doctor came to my room. He seems very frustration over my bloodpressure, that was something I could read through his, opinion even if I understand the frustration of the doctor I didn`t see that my own living was a problem even if it provably was a bigger problem, I dont want to see it. After the round the doctor sign me out, and wanted me to go to the pharmacy to buy out some medicin. It was a good thought, but unfortunately there came other between. My old life reminds me, and I was going again despite my bloodpressure. Now when I`m sitting and write those inroads I see how bad it really was. My mobilphone started to ring, in normal order, and it should be a warningsign for me but unfortunately not.

Chapter 3: Back again

Fairly soon I was back in my destructive life. The people
in my entourage have to except me, to conduct to my obligations. Even if it means that I would play with my own
life, I never holded back.
I believe that you are fairly strange if you think like that, I
should have thought different, but I didn`t, anow it hurts,
when I´m thinking about it. Of cours I should think about
my children, and my grandchildren before I went back to
my old life. You understand I didn´t. I coating barely came out from the hospital, the negative people were round
me, the people I shouldn`t ought with.

Directly I wonder what they has to sell. The problem with
mobilphones the want to sell is that you must have a
buyer to the hole batch. I haven´t got any bayer to the
batch. It was an awfully, awfully strange feeling that I
have, and couldn´t put my finger on. A feeling hows not
gonna be here. Anyway my reptilebrain thought that it
could be much money. I dont understand I could think
that way, when I´m siting and writing this inroads. My
weekday went out on that other persons and people have
to carry through different forms of crime. Had I´ve been
that apathetic, that I dont care about other people. Maybe
it was like that, the feeling was. Had I´ve got empathy for
other people maybe or it just a feeling that I have. Well
what do I know.

It was a fairly brittle feeling for me. But what the hell can I do about it, not that much. I had enough people around me every day, people who expect that I have to conduct my obligations. I need to talk to different people all the time so the activities could roll on in an ordinary way. I´ve notice, that I start getting old for this shit. The cockerels have another kind of energy to accomplish to this shit. I´ve notice that I´m not in the same shape, as before. The cockerels can go on the hole night, and even if I felt that I have to sleep, wasn´t that an option. My body don´t accept this anymore, the question were for how long I had to manage. The worse is, the body have said from. This wasn´t anything I thought would happend in my career. Well, it provably have done, even if I dont want to accept it. I am more tired for every dag, and the cockerels notice, that I am more tired since my heartat-tack. The cockerels want to facilitate my weekday.

Chapter 4: Lassitude

The cockerels helped me every day, I felt tired, and it started to spread like ripples, with the heartattck I´ve had. I didnt´t have the same driv I had before. It was hard to take, that I couldnt do the same declarations in the same rate I use to. I thought it was annoying to see that I´m to old for this shit. Like they always say, you should stop when you´re on the top. The question, I really ask myself was, if I really reached the famous top, so I could stop with all the shit criminality amount to. My own children who hasen´t got the time they really earned. To call yourself a dad, it´s a big joke, if you at the same time, have to keep on to crime actions. I couldn´t understand that I really do that, I couldn´t be a good father and make crime actions according the law. Anyway, I´ve started to think about quit with all the shit, and spend some time on my children and grandchildren like a father and a grandpa would do. Spend some time with the children, who were worth having their dad, who set inside, and served his intence. The thought was good, and I really want to do that, even if it´s gonna be difficult with kiddo gravel. I had a feeling that it`s gonna be big troubles, I dont want any problems, it have to be flexible. It´s gonna be to prepare an exit, without anyone being acerb or disappointed, even if it´s gonna be a hard declaration, I was willing to try. Talk about that I´m asked for trouble, I just could quit like you see, but I was fast determined to try in a little scale. I want to do clear my dealings, before I ´ll act. I know, I thought in the evening how it´s gonna go if I quit. My children was in focus when I thougt about my future.

Chapter 5: Tompa

I meet Tomba in the morning, and I suspect that he may
think that I would stop with the criminal bite. I´ve noticed
of the acting he had, or was I paranoid. We waited for the
customers to come and buy the mobilphones we had,
Tompa did not say that much, he was suspected against
me.

The customers arrived, in a fairly decent car, and after
that car, it was an old Iveco, it looks like a bus, were they
problaby would have the mobilphones they bought from
us. We didn´t know, we were just speculated. Two men
came out of the car they arrived in, they were fairly nice,
however, they dont want to pay that much for the mobilphones we wanted. It´s gonna be another negotiation about
what they`re gonna pay for the mobilphones. Before the
dealing ends, the buyers told us what they want to pay for
the mobilphones, that price were not current anymore for
them. They want to pay 15 % less. I thinking about, if I
should sell for their price so I get rit of the shit, and to be
excused the criminal shit, at the same time Tompa want
so much money thats possible for the mobilphones, so it´s
been a moment 22 between me and Tompa. It´s ended
that I had to go away and talk with Tompa individually.
You dont wanna discuss this when the possible buyers
can hear. Tompa was fairly arranged about what he want
for the mobilphones, he was fairly hard to dally with, and
fairly convinced.

I have my own thoughts about the criminal bite and how I gonna end with it, and I couldn´t tell Tompa.

The question is, how I would convice Tompa to sell the mobilphones 15 % cheaper then we said from the start, and whats the reasons why I will sell for cheaper. I didn´t know what I should tell him for reason to sell for less. I could´t tell him directly that I´m gonna quit, that would probably make him some disappointed, or pretty much. After the discussion with Tompa, the price be 15 % cheaper than the baseprice from the start. Of cours the buyers be happy for the notification. They probably already have buyers for the mobilphones to another price then we have at the beginning. The buyers also want to make on this deal. We started to load in the mobilphones in the truck the other two men came in. Said and done, they drove thence, and I and Tompa could go back to our sheet. I actually went home after we been at the sheet. I felt that was very amiss, I had suffered by something called old age. I simply begin being to old for this shit. Tompa were ten to eleven year, younger than I and have another energy than I. He wanted and had the drive to make money. Above all he have the energy I didn´t, so it was easier for him.

I parked my car outside the house and, went in, I have a fairly harmless eye, and have a lots off thoughts about how my life could be if I really quit with this shit. There was some stuff I have to clear up if I should stop, above all I dont want to come in a bad daylight, which many does when they stop with criminalty. I want above all that my own children and Anna which I have the children with

should live the unaffected life, that doesn´t have any ne-gative filling, even if I choose to resign my negative life.
I get more and more used to the thought that I´m gonna to resign and quit my criminal life, even if it´s gonna affect me with negative sense, I ve decided to do that. The strange thing about it all, is that I am on my own has to make this decision, there were absolutly no one to advise my in this question. I stand fairly alone with this decision, the question was, if it´s gonna to favour, if I choose to quit, or I would experience something negative with my choice.

I have hopes to see my children, as a normal father would do, if I quit this shit. I`ll even realize that it would affects me in a negative form in the beginning, the question was for how long, it would be negative when I not can see my children for a while. I´ve asked myself, if I`m gonna fix it if it´s be negative, and will my family handle the situati-on, or just turn the back on me.

My children Alex and Tobias were in focus all the time, and like the most of you know, you´re not stronger than the weak link, and my family were the weakness in my life. So the question I`ve asked myself was, if it were worth to quit or I should go on with the negative life, to make any contact with my children. The fact is, that my children is something you´re proud of us a father, even if my children not can be proud of their father, who had meant a lot of boredom, arrests, jail sentences as a relati-onship consisted of. I wasn´t directly proud for this frame of references, but it´s actually that world my children we-re used to.

Chapter 6: Possibilities

I have different thoughts of different scenarioo, that could
aff me negative or positive depends on the choice I made.
The question is just, which choice I´m gonna do. The fact
is that irrespective which choice I make, it´s gonna be
negative for some people and positive for some. If I turn
on this situation it will be exactly on the contrary, where
the other part will be haunted.

Honestly I think it was an awfully difficult choice to
make, and it will probably affect me on a negative way no
matter what I did. The fact is, that I have to make a choice
even if I dont want to. I asked the persons who were close
to me, how I´m gonna do in this situation, and believe me
there wasn´t anyone who want to do any choice, or
recommend something to me, probably it depends on the
built in fear the person had. There was one person who
were very close to me, and actually gave me fairly good
advice so I could see the situation with new eyes. When
I´m looking at the situation with other eyes, and other
facts, the state is different, even if it was wise word from
the person concerned, I realize on my own that it probably
would be iffy. The word were wiegh heavy, but other persons could see it negative, even if it´s gonna be a positive
direction for me.
So I had to make a decision on the issue, the question
was, how would Tompa and Wilson receive such a decision? Their income would deteriorate sharply.

Chapter 7: Wilsons family

Wilson himself had a family with two children and a girl so there would probably not be a problem with him. Tompa, on the other hand, was a pretty unheard of card where I did not know how to accept this. I had my family to think about, and I had a very good reputation in the lower world so why ruin it. Tompa could actually be a rather powerful problem, something I had to wonder with.

I realized that I once again was too old for this shit and I really wanted to quit, now only some people who would be convinced of this were something I did not know for the time being how to do. The fact was that I would make a choice, no matter what consequences it might be, so I was determined to make a choice. I started already the next day to work out by planning the business we had before us, I had to finish in a smooth and smart way without anyone suspicious. In the evening, I went to our warehouse where we had the next delivery hard disks that we would send away to new buyers, it was SCSI hard disk drivers with cabling. We had about 50 hard disks that would replace owners, the question I put myself when I stood in front of these hard disks, if I could defend the risk that obviously existed if we were to be taken into action as opposed to not carrying out this deal.

I did not think I wanted to take the risk, probably it was my bad conscience that remind me. I knew that Tompa would come in the morning, or the morning after, he had a vision of how he wanted it to end, he was completely focused on making money, that's the only thing he thought of day and night. Tompa was a very kind and humble person in general, but he had some tendencies to want to use violence and I also felt a weakness with him. They say that you get wiser over the years, the older you become, and sad enough, although some people would make a lot of money that absolutely was not wrong, you have to look at the risks and consequences that can be caused by negative things should happen. Tompa was not a person who saw these consequences as a risk, he lived absolutely for the day, it was probably so I had lived in my young days. So I knew I had to do something about this matter on my own.

I started thinking about what I would do, now it was quite urgent, that this shop would happen within a few days, so I had to act on the question. I thought that they were a rather hard thought, when I thought about it, at the same time, I thought I was a little sorry for Tompa who looked forward to this deal. Had my empathy gained a foothold or not, anyway, I did not know what I exactly would do. The questions were many, and they did not light up directly with their presence, so I began to wonder, if a car battery was the solution to my problem. Everyone who is using computers, knows that a hard drive that would have a power kiss, stops working. I went and picked up a car battery, two cables I started scaling off at both ends, so I could put them on the plus and the minus poles. Then I gave a hard drive an electric shock to see if it worked, then I took the hard disk, rewritten it and mounted it in a computer on the store as slavish to see if it started. I was pleased to note that the hard drive was dead, then I uninstalled it, went back and put it on the pallet again. When the hard drive did not work, I gave other hard disks an electric shock, now a problem was resolved. Then I gone home, and waited the next day, before I went back to our warehouse. Tompa was already there, when I got there the day after, he was excited to see if the buyers took all the hard drivers he had imagined.

I came into our warehouse, Tompa talking to another person, whom I dont know who it was. I went to Tompa, he started presenting the other person as Harald, and he also said that Harald was possibly a future businessman. More would not Tompa say so go on that occasion, it was more his eyes that said the more, I knew him pretty well since before, so it would be fun to hear what he had to say about the person in question.

I went back into what we called the office, it consisted of four walls, a cardboard and a computer, more it was not for a offices. Tompa entered the office after talking to Harald, Tompa said he seemed quite confident, himself I said I do not think so much because I do not know the person in question, and you dont know him so much, that you can say that he is trustworthy. Tompa probably got a little angry with me, because we had two different opinions about how a person who was trustworthy was. As a result, Tompa raised his voice quite a bit, and told her position in this matter to me clearly and clearly.

There was nothing that I cared about much about. Me and Tompa were divorced as less good friends, and one thing was done, we could agree that we did not agree.

The clock began to get closer to twelve, and I did not actually find Tompa, we would within a couple of hours carry out a fairly big deal that Tompa was looking forward to. Now he was not demonstrable, and I did not really find him. I wondered clearly how to do, as a person to stay away, when you could stay away when we were doing a fairly big deal, he would have been totally indifferent over this deal, or was he just cursed by our discussion that we had earlier in the day. Luckily, I done it with the hard drive the night before, which mean, I had some time left, I could only wait for Tompa to come back. Is it something you do when you have a lot of time left to think and think, which I had now, I once again began to think about my family, and if I would make an end to this once and for all.

Just when I was thinking about the most, Tompa returned, he was a bit annoyed, and I noticed that he had a certain attitude and that was nothing I liked right away. We had about 40-45 minutes to drive, before we got to the place where the deal would be made up, and it was a little more than an hour left before the buyer came, it was a fairly prevailing silence that was between me and Tompa, probably wondering Tompa why I did so, and I wondered why he did as he did. We had about a quarter left after we had drove off, and had now stayed our car, I knew that our hard drivers would not work, something that Tompa did not cope with. The buyer came and wanted to test a hard drive, which was not directly unusual, you would not buy the pig in the bag, and he would not.

He took one of the hard drives, left for about twenty minutes and came back there, then told that the hard drive wasn´t working, it was completely dead. Then Tompa said, you can put it back and take a few others and try them, as he did. He left and came back after half an hour, again he came to us and said that the hard drives are also completely dead, they do not work at all. Tompa and I started looking at each other, I had to play in this fox as it was, I knew the hard drives were broken, I knew I had given them an electric shock, that was something that Tompa did not totally had a clue, and in this racing game I did not have either. As a result, the buyer resigned after returning the rugged hard drivers. Tompa, on the other hand, was really pissed off, because he believed that the people we bought them from had fooled us, by giving us wrong and rugged hard drives. It became quite difficult for me to hold back Tompa, for now he was really pissed of, he probably wanted the seller to meet his creator. For my part, it was difficult to calm him down at the same, time as I knew it was me who had ruined the hard drives.

Tompa went off to calm down, myself sat in the car and waited for Tompa to take it a little quieter. It seemed quite difficult to get Tompa calm again, he simply wanted revenge, and I did not think I was good. It was only for my part to hope that he had calmed down until the day after for now it was impossible to calm him down. We went and took a coffee so that "we" could calm down, it had been a bad day, purely business-related, where we only had a pile of bad hard drives that a profiteous maniac had fooled us.

There were not so many words said where we sat at the billboard, Tompa was angry and I pretended to be angry. At the same time, I felt that my inner smile would be reminded, but it was not, an alternative in this situation.

We got ready, after we got up, we went back to the car, I drove home Tompa until his apartment, and let him down. We said bye to each other, then I went home to myself. In the evening I had some time left, and then all the thoughts began to grind, the girl I was with at the moment like all the other girls would talk about how to do. I replied that I'm crazy, HOW DO YOU GET? "I asked. It became quite, quiet because she probably did not expect me to answer anything, as I did. Like all other women, she can be quite mean, they do not know her own best, and then situations arise like it did now. I was pretty hard to focus on what was important, at the moment, I was thinking about Tompa quite a bit, even though it had hit him badly, so I had to do that, and I did not, I had never begun the first step in my execution. It was clear that I was wondering if it was right, especially against Tompa, Wilson and others.

In the evening when we went to bed, all the thoughts started again, they simply started to bother me, that was so negative, so I did not even want to think about it, even if it was just the focus on this problem. As I've always said before, the brain must handle all the information you have, even if you do not want to. It always works, as long as you sit on the cap, then it will be a problem when you lift the lid, which is, when you have to start handling the situation in its entirety. It was a problem that hit me now, and I had to deal with the situation in an objective way. My children and my family expected me to fix and solve it.

In the morning when I woke up, I went up and made arrangements, then I put on some coffee, and served some breakfast on the table, the girl I was together with just then came and sat at the table, she did not say much, on the other hand, her look said more. When she chose to say something, she clearly asked how I felt, and what I was going to do during the day. Nothing I replied, as little as possible, she noticed that I was a bit indifferent even though I did not want to be it. I felt more like I stood between heaven and hell, where I had to make a choice, a choice that I would not do under any circumstances. It was something that really took energy of me, when I thought about it. The girl sitting at the breakfast table began to talk about our coming future, it was a topic that was totally uninteresting to discuss for the moment. I could not even understand how this person could focus on something that was not a problem, at least not now and for me at all. I walked from the breakfast table into the big room, so I could be comfortable with my thoughts and thoughts. I thought my day had started in a negative way, and I would rather go to bed and forget all the thoughts I had. It was a very difficult choice I had in front of me, and there really was just more questions the more I figured. I went out and sat in the car and drove down to our warehouse, I had to come up with a smart and constructive solution so no person could suspect anything that I would end up with the flag. When I came down to our store, Lotti, Wilson's girl called, wondering where Wilson was, when he told Lotti that he would only do some small cases in the village and come home late.

Chapter 8: Wilsons Woman

Now I had his love on the thread, and I had to lie or relieve the truth, when I knew Wilson would be in for the next delivery we had today. It was Wilson and I who would carry out this store today, which consisted of delivering bells, 1800 pieces. There were quite a few preparations we had, and a lot of energy was required for it to work and we could carry out the deal. Wilson had his family to think about, not least his children as he had two of, and a future wife, who apparently would have a right side at Wilson.

I understood that these business could not continue in the same direction as before, given that Lotti would reverse Wilson in total. Me and Wilson prepared the deal by quality assuring some of the watches so that the customer could pay more for them. The thing was that we wanted to spend as much money as possible, which is quite normal. Lotti was wondering where Wilson got all the money from, and was on the track unfortunately. He had clearly explained to Lotti, that he had worked with various consultancy assignments for different companies, and could earn a lot of money in this way. Just a thought! Lotti was more of the skeptical variety, she had also asked me, if I knew where Wilson could get as much money as he had without any work. I always told her that I did not know how he earned his money. She said that she knew that Wilson and I were quite frequent and moved in pretty nice environments. The fact that Lotti had become a bigger problem for us was a fact, which we usually always had, and she usually questioned the most we did. But like all the other times, we did not know anything, it was nothing she immediately said, but probably she did not believe in any vocal or consonant as we said.

Back again to the story...

I picked up a lot of watches and looked at these, then looking at Wilson, we did not have any knowledge about this. So it was difficult to put a certain amount of value on the different watches; it became more that we got the hype for knowledge we absolutely did not have in this area. We start packing all the bells in a box, so that we could quickly access them if needed, if any buyer wanted to watch them. After we had packed them, we started loading them in the truck so we could drive away into the city. We could possible meet a buyer at a gas station outside the city, who was quite interested in these watches.

Me and Wilson sat in the truck, waiting for the possible buyer to come, when it rolled in a policecar. Obviously, they would have coffee at this gas station where we could possibly make up the deal. Now there was no current situation right away, we were kindly seated waiting for the possible buyer to show up so we could decide another place as it would not be appropriate to do that on this gas station. Wilson got hungry when we sat there waiting for the possible buyer, he went to buy a baguette with sausage, when the policemen were in there. He stood in a queue, and in front of him stood the cops, he would like to have his sausage. The longer time, Wilson became the more hungry, which meant he probably took large pieces of the sausages of the petrol station. When Wilson arrived at the checkout, one of the policemen sat by the side to get his hamburger that was not ready for the moment.

Wilson was not immediately pleased that this police was there. Wilson knew that our truck was full of stolen watches and he stood by a police waiting for his hamburgers to get ready. The fun in all this, is that the policeman, begins to converse with Wilson on general things, he wondered what he was doing there tonight, and asked a little fun if the lady had sent him. Well, Wilson said, I'm just hungry so I had to buy some food, the police understands more than well, if you're hungry, you are. It all ended with Wilson paying at the checkout and leaving with a smile on his lips. Wilson went back to the truck and told me about the whole incident with the cops, all of which ended we laughed heartily. Just a thought! So there are two cops in a gas station waiting for their burgers, and outside there is a lot of money for theft. Talk about these policemen are blown to the confection on the contrary.

After a while, the potential buyer came, Wilson left the truck and talked to them in the car, they were three. Wilson then briefly summarized that the cop was in the gas station, and there was no way to make up the business here. It all ended with Wilson telling us that we had to move a little bit, and asked the eventual buyers to drive after us in their car, as they did. I drove to another place, that lay a bit outside a forest, quite a good place, but I did not know where I was. It was a good place we found thought the buyers. Wilson jumped on the wreck and took some watches, some exclusive and some ordinary less worth the watches.

The buyers began to look at these watches, one of them took a magnifying glass or a lap of some kind, and began to look at the watches; after a while watching these watches, he spoke with the other colleague that some watches were of high quality and others were low-cost. The other colleague then said that they only wanted quality watches, such watches that cost 7-8000 for what their customers wanted. This would mean in a round a store around 315,000 swedish crowns, which would also mean that I and Wilson had about 900 low budget watches that we did not get rid of for the moment. The customer received 900 pieces of watches. Me and Wilson had 900 other issues that were the remaining low budget watches, that were and which we did not get rid of.

Chapter 9: Location Selection

The question was just what we would do now, and where we were going to put the watches in a safe place. We thought we would sell all the watches to this buyer, so unfortunately we did not get the case, and we had a problem, we had to solve, and today. The buyers paid the watches in cash and left therefrom.

Both me and Wilson should have been happy, but we did not, as we said, we had another problem to solve, putting these low budget watches in a good and safe place. We only came to the fact that we could restore the watches to our warehouse.

Then it became ... We came back with the truck into the warehouse that we had, and now it was just the question of where we would put the watches, at the same time Lotti called on, Wilson's mobile phone, wondering where he was. Wilson just looked at me, and giving me a look that's out of this world, I realized it was Lotti when he answered the phone just like he did. -Hallo Lotti, so I would understand it was her. Now there was another problem, now I had to put my phone silent if my phone would ring, and then she would understand that Wilson was with me. There was no alternative, then she would ask me again what we had done. It was enough for Wilson to talk to her, and calm her down in the best possible way. Wilson talked about Lotti for about twenty minutes and probably she got a bit calmer, it's nothing I know, but it seemed like Wilson, he also got calm, or he was just shocked, only scientists know.

We were back at our warehouse, and I was lucky to drive the car, when Lotti had a long conversation with Wilson. Once inside our store, I began to wonder where we would put this pallet with watches that we unfortunately had with us. Wilson also considered this problem. Just when we stood thinking about this problem, Tompa came. He understood that we had brought some watches back with us. Even he started to wondering where we would put our pallet with a lot of watches that would be put in such a way that no one could find it.

Wilson had found a great place to put that pallet on, so nobody could find it. Behind a pallet position he thought we could put it safely. Both me and Tompa went to look at this place. In fact, it was a good place where no one would even suspect we had placed these watches. We decided all three, because it was a good place so we went back to the truck to lift the pallet. Now we were three people, so it was not really that heavy lifting this pallet. Once we had taken it down from the truck we had a small pallet puller that we could drive the pallet to the place Wilson had found. When we got there, just bark it off the pallet carrier and fix it. To then pull the pallet in front of the pallet so nobody saw it. Now we were ready for the day. Wilson wanted to go home to her girlfriend. Probably they had more they needed to talk about. He would at least go home to Lotti and the children.

Chapter 10: Brain bleeding

Tompa did not have a girl, but he wanted to go home anyway. I myself had my job, and all the expectations that different personalities had on me. When I sat down to rest, it hurts in the pump (heart), once again the pump remind me of the heart attack I had. I had been offered Nitroglycerin for vasculature by the doctor, I said no.

In the evening, me and Tompa gonna do a job together. But at the moment, it felt like I needed rest. I fall asleep in the chair in the office so tired I was. There I sleept for four hours and Tompa, who was going to join the next job, wake me up. I did not even hear him coming into the room. When Tompa woked me up me, we would go to the next job. I was terribly tired and could easily sleep longer. Unfortunately, this did not work. Tompa drove the car, we entered a hotel we used to do. Before we went to check-in, I felt something was wrong with my body. It wasn´t something I wanted to talk to Tompa about at the moment.

We went to check-in and there were quite a nice staff who were of female sex. We got our passes by the check in staff and went to the elevator which would take us up to the floor we had received our room on. We arrived at the door and Tompa entered his passport so we entered our hotel room as we rented. Once inside the hotel room, I felt something was really wrong with me. My body did not want the same thing I do.

Probably, I had my bleeding in the cerebellum already, and my blood pressure was probably too high because there had been some evidence. Tompa wondered clearly how I felt when I was not talking directly.

My fine motor, was out of this world. Tompa experienced me more like being unwell, knowing that I had not been drinking alcohol since 1999, and thought it was a little odd considering the behavior that I had. Tompa, of course, wanted me to go to the hospital because I felt like I did, that's nothing I wanted to do. Tompa was probably quite worried when I had not responded to all his appeals as he did, I behaved in a very strange way. I felt that I probably should have gone to a hospital although I did not think for the moment that we had time with this in view of the upcoming business we had. But Tompa was apparently a pretty stubborn individual and wanted us to go to the hospital so I could be examined by a doctor.

When we arrived at the hospital, I probably was halfway unconscious or rather beaten. I know that I spewed quite vigorously before entering the emergency room. Tompa had gone before talking to the nurses and they walked and met me in the door, they probably understood that there was a stroke or similar discomfort that I had received. I entered the examination room directly, the nurses did not want me to sit or stand up, they wanted me to go to the bunk, but I did not want to. I know that those nurses made me sit in the bunk, I was quite hard with my balance, I looked more like a living ECG where I sat and swung with my bad balance. I only struggle against, and did not want to be unconscious under any circumstances, it proves impossible unfortunately. Oh, how bad it was to keep my eyes open so I could keep the check. Talk about an impossible mission!

Once again my nurses wanted me to lay down, because I could not sit straight as they would like. I know that they raised the bunk so I could half down, I know that my children Tobias and Alexander were the last thing I thought of, I could see my children in front of me, even though I now know that I only saw them in my mind. Probably that was where I totally lost consciousness, because then everything was dark.

According to statements, the following occurred:

Once I had lost my consciousness, a doctor entered the examination room, sending me directly to the X-ray where they determined that I had a cerebrovascular bleeding of a serious nature. Now it was damn fast, so I would not be a vegetable. As a result, the doctor sent me to a large hospital for surgery. The doctor had called so an ambulance arrived and came and picked me up once, then followed a few miles until I reached the big hospital where I was operated. All the time the doctors had a big pressure, so I would not get permanent but of this.
There were two doctor team, and they operated me for six hours. Where they had to tighten my head, cut half the head, and half my neck to knock holes so they reached the cerebellum and could suck out the blood that expanded heavily due to the bleeding, where a vessel had broken.

I can say now afterwards, that they are incredibly skilled the doctors, who perform this operation in a certain amount of time. Otherwise, you become a living vegetable and there is no alternative. Then the responsible physician decided that I would remain sore because of the swelling that had occurred between the cerebellum and the cerebral cortex, since it is not a good option when they are gathered due to swelling.

Chapter 11: Doctor's statement

The doctor thought it was better for me to be swept so that the swelling could go down by itself. I was sown for about a month so that the swelling could go down. My boys Tobias and Alexander were in and talked to the doctor, they had come from Skåne (Landscape in Sweden) up to Linköping because they wanted to be with their dad. I now know that Tobias was in the wheelchair at the moment and had difficulty walking because he had fallen down from a position. Alexander then, got put on this wheelchair when they got out of the hospital, it would go and eat pizza. They were looking for a pizzeria, which made them discover that there was a pizzeria above the park. This caused the little boy Alexander to face the challenge of his life; they would pass a high hill and Alexander had to put Tobiah's wheelchair. Now it was only that Alexander was as coarse as Skinny Jim, that is, he had no muscles at all. So the back they faced became a challenge without its similar to Alexander. Once they got up on the hill, it was only a few hundred yards to the pizzeria, probably Alexander was reddish of this great challenge he had done. When they got into the pizzeria they were allowed to order, both of them wanted a kebab pizza with garlic dressing, then the pizzeria owner said in breaking Swedish:

-We have no garlic dressing, we make our own dressing. This made the boys in common answer: -WHAT? Then Alexander asked in his language: -have you no garlic dressing?

Then the pizza replied the owner, who did not understand, so well, that he thought they would try his dressing, it was quite good, said the pizza owner. The guys were quite hesitant trying this dressing, but they did it anyway. The guys were probably not that interested pizza owner's sauce ... The guys thought it was a pretty good dressing when they tasted it, even if it was not of garlic character.

The guys went back to the hospital when they had eaten their pizzas and the realm was unfortunately a completely different one. They did not think it was good, that their dad was in the hospital, so they tried to make the most of the situation. The little boy Alexander had his work to think about, and he had his girl he was with, who would come up the next day. Tobias, who is the silent kind, did not say much, not at least as much as Alexander said, they were two different guys, who acted on the emerging situation in completely different ways. The doctor would talk to them again about how big the chances their dad had to survive this stroke. The boys entered the doctor's room and they could see their father's brain on the picture with the swelling, that pushed the brain cortex due to the surgery.
The doctor said, -If your dad survives the weekend, there is a pretty good condition for him to survive. It was the weekend that was absolutely crucial how their father's life would be, the doctor told them.

The guys probably gone out and talked, and were determined that the following weekend was quite crucial how
their father's life would be. The boys sat with their father
for the whole weekend, and wondered exactly what would
happen to him, and if they had his father in life. Probably
it was quite tiring thoughts that they had, and that probably demanded quite a lot of energy when they sat thinking about it. As you said, they were completely different
as people, but whatever their father would be, they would
be able to finish the weekend before them. I know now
afterwards when I talk with the guys that time went
awfully slow for them, every minute was like a day as
they said, and I can really understand that. Then it would
be quite crucial to their future if it went wrong and they
lost their Daddy. The guys had most likely managed a life
without their father. For the moment, it was not so, but the
boys had to plan for the worst even if they dont want to.

In the evenings they were at the hospital hotel, they had
for, thoose who had been operated, who has to stay for a
long time. During the days, they had to buy breakfast for
a lesser cost, then they had to talk to the curator that the
hospital have.

The guys had a lot of questions that were of a fairly natural nature. It's not easy to get answers to all the questions
you have, when your parent is in a hospital and is being
put to sleep. I can really understand now, that the guys
had very many decisions to take. Tobias had her girl and
children to think about, not mentioning the job he had.

Both the boys had a job, so they did not go straight into his father's footsteps, thankfully, they had gone more in the mother's footsteps. But all the conversations with a doctor and curator, it was a fact that I had survived the weekend, it was over. Even though I was sore and alive, the doctor did not know if I had any damage to this stroke. The guys asked several times as themselves said, how it would be for the old man, and the doctors said it was very hard to say, which might be because their father was anesthetized. The doctor kept me ashamed because my body healed faster then. Tobias had a couple of conversations from her girl who wanted him to stay for as long as he wanted to be with his dad. Probably it became quite difficult to stay for him, because of his work where they needed him. Tobias thought it was a very difficult decision to make, he had to go home for his job, even though he would like to stay with his dad. Alexander had a girl, who supported him in this, but he also had his work to think about, when he had a managerial service so both guys had a hard decision to take, even if they would like to stay with their dad, unfortunately this did not work. Now, afterwards, I know that I was in a state of sleep for almost a month, which caused the nurses who cared for me to write a diary so that I would not spend a whole month when I was being sly. The decision of the boys to go home was correct because of that.

After a month the Doctor decide to take the drugs away so I could wake up at my own pace to avoide that the patient get scared or get hypertension which not good when you had a stroke. I woke up and try to get oft he bed.

Under my mattress there was another mattress, which was thinner and had a sensor us alarmed to the personal if I would lift from the bed.

Now there was just a little problem, I couldn`t move my left side, it was totally gone which is an ordinary affliction by a stroke. Apparently I had a pretty good force in my right hand, which made that I could heel me over the bed rail to get out of there. The results is that I came over the bed, put off the drip in my arm, which starts bleeding, I fall at the floor, broke my head and it bleeding yet more. The floor was filled when the nurses came. The alarm had started when I left the mattress and they came in about 10-15 seconds after. There was probably much blood which came from the drip. It`s become a big pull when the nurses came and saw all the blood on the floor.

The Doctor been contacted by the nurses who want that I will be x-ray, so I diden`t get other damages when I`ve fallen. The nurses dried up all blood on the floor and put on some bandage so the blood will stop.

When you have a stroke you get some anticoagulants and it`s not so good to broke the head when the bleeding can be hard to stop, because of the medicin.

When the nurses laid me back in my bed, the doctor entered my room. He wanted me to go to X-ray, then I answered: No I do not want to. The doctor then said he would make sure I had not received any new damage be

cause of the case, but again I said, I did not want it. The doctor can not resist what the patient wants, even though he looked quite frustrated at my decision, that was the case.

The doctor had to go, he had more patients he had to make sure, he finished this visit by pointing out the importance of being x-rayed, then he left. The male nurse then came into my room and once again declared that they wanted me to X-ray me. According to mine, they were half a day, so I had to give up on their cheats. They drove me on the X-ray, and it took about ten minutes later I was done, honestly, then X-ray was very loud. When I finished, the nurses returned me to my room.

In the afternoon, the doctor returned to my room explaining that he had looked at the X-rays and was able to determine that I did not incur any new damages due to the case. The doctor and I thought that was very good. My guys often called the department, and wondered how their dad did, it was nothing I knew about at the time, that was something I found out afterwards. For every day that went, I was pretty convinced I was better, but unfortunately I did not get it. My blood pressure and my blood fat was too high as the doctor said, and he would prescribe some other medications so I would fix my problem. Now it meant rehabilitation for my part. The physiotherapists came and picked me two to three times a week from my room, and I had to sit in a wheelchair and get driven to the gymnastics department where I would work out to go in a ribbon chair.

Chapter 12: The Physiotherapists

They put on me a red belt around my waist with handles
so that they could hold me if I would fall, they would start
the signals between the brain and the legs. I know they
put such a belt on me, I think I went three steps late, I was
tired like a retirement home and did not want to go anymore. I had to go back and put me in my wheelchair then
drove them back to my room, they helped me in bed, then
I slept for about twelve hours. As you said, you get very
tired after a stroke, and for those who do not know what
brain fatigue is, I'll explain it. It's almost like you'll get
postprandial somnolence when you had eaten and getting
tired.
When you are brain-tired, it's about as badly as hell, it's
brain-tired hot. Something that I often reflected on was,
that I did not get any visits either from Wilson or Tompa,
only from my family. I thought quite often why that was
so, but I actually do not know why, now afterwards I've
asked myself why it became as it became, but unfortunately nobody knows.

Just a thought!
My own theory, is that you do not want to disturb someone when such a situation has incurred, you probably do
not know how to handle it, or what to talk about. My
whole life had now become that I wanted to return to a
very ordinary smith life. That one could not do that which
creates a frustration for me, which does not matter to ho-
es. I really tried to rehabilitate myself in such a way that I
would have the opportunity to come back to an ordinary
life.

Back to my life story...

Even though I did not have any visits, I was terribly stubborn, I have told myself to do this, even if it would be difficult to succeed, I was sure I would try in any case.

Monday to friday there was rehabilitation of different way. I once know that two speech therapists came to my room and picked me up because I would be subjected to different scenarios, I had to go with them in a wheelchair and get into their office as they had. I rolled to a table where there is something short-like object, the speech therapist says as following: I will read a scenario for you and we want you to solve it in the best possible way. The scenario was as follows: Jesper, you get the following scenario, you come home and your entire home is filled with water, what are you doing? My reptile brain receives the following message: I call the plumber, knocks down my neighbor, take his wallet and take the money out and pay the plumber. Then, the speech therapist says: -So do not make Jesper, you should do the following: put on the boots, shut the water, call the plumber, have an invoice, you should have done Jesper. Then I answered: -It had become too expensive. When the speech therapist talked to me, she drove me back to my room, and when I was sitting in my room, thinking that was a pretty good solution to the problem, but the speech pedagogy did not like it. But that's how life is, we have different solutions to any problems.

I had to lay in my bed, and there were always a nurse in
my room, if I wanted to go to bed so she could help me.
The nurse asked me if I wanted to take a shower the next
morning, and I thought that was a good idea. Before she
left, she asked if she would turn on TV, and I thought that
was a good suggestion.

When you had a Stroke, it's very common to look twice as
I did, and it's always fun if there's a woman in front of me
and not a man when you look twice. The head of department came into my room and asked if I wanted a patch for
the eye because I look double and if I wanted earplugs, I
said that I would like a patch to look like a pirate patch,
and it was much easier to look at TV. Unfortunately, only
a woman was, but that's what one can live with. During
the rest of the hospital, my life consisted of sleeping and
rehabilitation.

The next morning I woke up and was terribly tired,
though I was about a meter up in the air with a lift, and
went to the shower. I entered the toilet in the harness because I could not walk after that, I would go into the
shower, and it was not easy, it was more difficult than
easy. There were two nurses who helped me when I went
into the shower, it was not so great for one nurse, she was
as beautiful as an early morning breeze so you would not
go to the shower right away. When I sat there in my solitude, wondering how this was going, considering that I
was completely lame on the left side. I got rid of me, and
then I had to take some soap and soap in and then I rinsed
off, it was really hard, an exercise that made me quite
tired. Then I told the nurses that I was ready. They helped
me out of the shower and sat on another chair in the
bathroom where I would put on my clothes. When I sat
there and would put on my clothes, I really understood

that this would be a big problem with big P. Put on clothes when you are completely lame on the left side, that is, it does not matter at all to put on their boxers shorts, did not get easy. The right side went pretty well, it was quite a big problem when you would put on the left side. After all the rules of the art, I finally got my boxer shorts after about twenty minutes. Then I had to call a nurse to put on my other clothes within a reasonable period of time. When I finished my clothes, I had to get the harness again so I would get up in bed. When I lay there in my solitude, I really thought that I take things for granted, that it should only work. I realized that I had a very long journey ahead of me that would mean many problems for me and that I had to adapt to them. Even when it looked quite dark, I have to say I had a real raw desire to get away from this hospital.

As I said earlier, I had no visits except for the family, now it was about to change completely because I was an organized criminal, who now had been internationally wanted. Then the police had contacted Wilson because he was vice president of one of the companies we had. Lotti, his girlfriend, had become quite frightened when the police had come, and had a visit with them and wanted to speak with Wilson individually, where they had explained that I, Jesper Persson, was internationally requested and that there was now a European arrest warrant on me. Probably Wilson became so nervous after the police conversation that they had with him, so he told the police what hospital I was in. Then they left from there and wished him a good

life, they had finally said that they would not have anything to do with me. The next day, the police came to the
hospital because they wanted to arrest me, the problem
was when the doctors and staff had a duty of confidentia-
lity, they did not even tell me I was there. When the police had talked to the doctor and the staff, the doctor went
to my room and asked what I thought he would say because I had an international inquiry on me. To me there
were only two choices, either I could tell the doctor that
he could not say anything, or I had to take the bull at the
horns. For my part, the later became the one I choose, to
take the bull at the horns and put an end to this. The doctor walks out of my room, and probably goes to the police
and requests them to enter his office, where he tells the
patient that he is at this department. It only takes half an
hour after the doctor had gone, and there are two cops in
my room. They saw, myself, that I was bad there and understood quite soon that I could not be moved from there.
They informed me that I would be moved to the detention
center as soon as it became appropriate to move me there
as the doctor said. Because it is the doctor who has the
main responsibility for his patient, not the police. What
the police can do is put two privately-run police outside
my room while I'm in the hospital. Because I was now
internationally requested, it became much more difficult
for my own part. In any case, the police put a police outside my room.

I soon understood that Wilson had made a statement because the police were looking for me at the hospital now.
It`s was probably quite crowded not to mention his fa-
mily, Lotti had been to him several times so he probably

had no choice. Now that the police were here, Wilson had his back free, he'd talked about where I was, and he was not even suspicious, and I thought that was a little strange. Since the Executive Vice President also has financial responsibility, the matter became strange in its entirety. During the next two days, I stayed in the hospital and then moved to the detention center using the police.

Chapter 13: The Prison

Once inside the detention, my problems started, the reality had come to me, and I sat on the enrollment, in the detention and I was unfortunately quite famous there. I did not need to immediately legitimize me, the detention personnel who came in knew who I was. The problem was that I could not touch my left side, and it took time to change clothes to fence clothes.

I now got to go, with the help of two guards (detention staff) to my cell inside the detention center. When I got into my cell it felt familiar, I had been there a few times. Pretty tired of writing these shit rows, considering that I have to think again of everything negative I have done. I'm on the hood and watching TV and feeling that there's something wrong with my body. I try to tell the guards to come to my cell. I'm also trying to get back quickly to bed because my balance is not so good at all. The waiting staff cries and asks what I wanted, and they knew I had come straight from the hospital. They told the speaker that they would get there as they did.

There was a woman and a man from the detention staff and asked how I was doing, then an executive officer came and asked him how I was doing. I answered the same as I told them others that there is something wrong, of which the executive commander decided to do, I would check what blood pressure was, which they did. It turned out that it was a little over 200 in blood pressure and 105 in lower blood pressure. When it turned out that I had so high blood pressure, the executive commanded the hospital information and asked what they would do.

The hospital information asked me if I had over 200 in blood pressure, yes, the executive commanded and he had a stroke, which meant that at the hospital information I had to go to the hospital immediately. The fun in all this, was that I just got from the hospital, and now they had to drive me back to the emergency room again. It turned out that I had too high blood pressure. It is the custody of a nutshell ... The ambulance arrived and blood pressure measurement was found to be too high. The ambulance driver started laying me on a British, so they could roll me up to the elevator. Inside the elevator it was quite crowded that did not go so fast, I was in the British, two ambulance drivers and a guard. So in a small elevator it became crowded. Probably it was not advisable to be such many people at the elevator. I must be glad that the lift stopped, because then it had become a little acid to breathe. Ambulance staff now put me in the stretcher in the ambulance. It was a lot of impressions I would take to myself, and someone who had just had a stroke might have a little hard to do with this. The hospital was just a stone's throw from the detention, so I had to change my mind quite soon.

Chapter 14: The Hospital

Once inside the department there were lots of samples and tests. It turned out that there was a more emergency department with a lot of emergency equipment, and a lot of monitors hanging in the air. The nurse came in and would take lots of samples so they knew what to do. The whole situation makes my heart beat a little extra. I probably was a little stressed about this. The samples proved was good. My blood pressure dont make, the doctor who came into the room so impressed. The doctor said he thought I would stay at the hospital for observation, so my blood pressure not get higher.

A nurse started rolling my bed to the elevator and then there came another nurse who helped. Once inside the elevator there was a guard too. We came up to the department where I would stay the night. The nurse rolled my bed into a room. It was a big challenge, and the guards began rolling down the window against the department so I could take it a bit quietly. The doctor who´s gonna investigate me came in, and he was a little worried about my health, since I had the stroke. It´s evening, and I had to go to bed. The two guards who went with me to the hospital would end for the day. One of them from the detention would remain overnight, and work over, while the other one would go home, which meant, that the executive command had to call another person who could be in the hospital during the night.

After half an hour there was a new guard that would be in the room during the night. It was a male guard that came to the room which seemed nice, he greeted me, so the ice was broken, so the worst was over.

I could hardly go because of the stroke I had, and it was quite difficult to get into the toilet when one of the legs felt heavy. Even if it was only two meters to the toilet, it was a full time job, once inside the toilet, it felt like a great freedom. Even that I knew there were two plits sat outside the door, that was the feeling I got. How a toilet can feel like a freedom. You could lock and unlock yourself even if it was guards outside the door. When I finished the toilet, I went to bed again. The guards asked if I wanted help, so I was not at that stage to get help from a guard. I was only at the beginning of my punishment, and I had been seventeen years in organized crime, so the answer was pretty much given ... thanks but no thanks. I thought it was quite difficult to sleep when there were two guards that would basically keep track of me. That they needed to be two picks to keep track of me is a mystery. I could barely go. So to run from the place was no alternative, I screwed most of me because there were quite a few thoughts that I had to be able to handle, not least the thought and feeling of getting Stroke.

I was in hospital, because I had high blood pressure, stressed and high blood pressure may cause Stroke. Sure, that feeling had got a foothold on me. It was a feeling that hurt me really. The night was like that and the sleep deficiency was loose with its presence. Soon it was morning, and the round was a fact. The doctor came in and asked if I wanted a beta blockers, something I definitely would not have. It feels like you get into a wall, when taking these pills. The doctor realized that I really did not want these pills, and did not prescribe such a thing.

He would, however, see how my blood pressure acted during the night and if I needed new medicine. The doctor went, and one the detention officer, said that he probably had 200 in blood pressure if he had also been convicted of such a long prison sentence.

At night, the reception staff would be awake, I was sleeping myself, I thought I was pretty nice, but I woke up every time someone went to the toilet of the detention staff.

In the morning, the doctor returned to the round and said that my blood pressure had gone down, with the medicine I had received, and he thought I could go back to the detention during the day. He did not feel any worries directly because of my blood pressure after the stroke I had. Responsible doctor thought my blood pressure was a bit high, but he was not worried. So I could go back to the detention center. Now it was the question of whether I needed handcuffs or not? A guard called the detention and asked if I would have handcuffs or not. It was decided that I did not need it so we went back to the custody again. Once upon a time, there were many thoughts I was thinking about. Not least on the Stroke I had. The question was, how to handle a lot of years on the pitcher. I could barely go, and now I was on the run. There was not much to do, there was a bed and a table with a chair stuck, in the table. There was a TV that stood up on the desk, then there were no more things. The guards helped me get rid of, as there was no alternative to standing up for me the day becomes heavy when I not could do anything.

Later in the day I had to go back to the detention with the staff, there came a car and picked us up from the detention. After 15 minutes we were back at the detention center.

It was the same routines again, but I had a fitting clothes so I did not have to change. I just wanted to come to an instution there are more human conditions there. But that was nothing that the placement device intended to fix. Even though, at this time, I had a location, so transport and shelter did not seem to be so sync. I had to sit four days before transport came and picked me up. As a reader you can think that four days goes quite fast. But to say that, is completely wrong. I thought that one hour was as long as a week.

Just a thought! Little later in the day my lawyer would come, and because there was no more to do on the judgment, my lawyer's visit was the social way. When he was leaving, he was going to take the elevator down, pushing the button and the elevator coming up, I return to my cell with the help of the suspension staff. My lawyer goes into the elevator, and going to trial, where he will be the defender of a client. The elevator stops just as he enters the elevator, so you see a slight slit up to the detention department. Then my lawyer finds out on the emergency signal and at the detention department, then the executive commands and looks into the elevator from above, then he told my lawyer to fix it, but he also said he would not go anywhere, while my Attorney more or less shake his head, and determined that he was, stuck in a lift.

After a few minutes my lawyer came out from there, the executive commander had got down the elevator so everything ended happily. My lawyer came to trial in time so he could defend his client. My lawyer was wondering why the Executive Commander was worried that he would leave the elevator when he got, stuck in it…………
Commentary superfluous!

Back to my life story!

Sitting in my cell, and thinking about life, and there is a proverb which is: **Don´t do the crime if you can´t take the time**. It's a little hard to defend that saying because I was deprived of liberty, so that word does not mean that much.

I asked the detention staff if I could not get to the community department, there you should not be sitting very often. Then they said that I would fill in a patch as the executive commander will make a decision, if I could sit with the grab gravel, or it was of the wrong color. It would have made me unable to sit there then.

The next day, I was moved to the G Department (Community Department), where there were some people, and some of them were really disturbed in the head of pure Swedish. Europe's largest human trafficker was there, the biggest card-haired was there, and some other tired drug addicts who only had drug abuse. There was quite a big difference to be sitting in that department, against sitting with restrictions in the cell twenty-three hours a day and with one hour's air a day.

In that department I sat about two days before I was moved to the cage (prison). In the morning there were four guards who would pick up two people from the detention center, that would be in the office. I could not even go, so the guards wanted to know what they could do to facilitate my stay at the detention center. The above event only proves that the prosecution has lost control of my case, before Justice Minister Beatrice Ask rejected my case, who said she had not even read my lawyer's paper.

She has probably only seen the grace application and then given a rejection. Her signature is witnessed, all of this just indicates that the rule of law is on decline. You can laugh like a Smith, and not care about the matter.

Probably you forget something that reads these lines ... It could hit you! Anyway!

Just a thought... It is quite strange how the rules are in the prosecution. If youdont are a person in a permit, the pledges shall imprison the person if they consider it necessary. Have talked with client manager Peter and coordinator Jörgen about what really matters if a person comes from the detention to a hospital. What are the rules that apply? According to the coordinator Jörgen, no general rule applies. It is from person to person who is detained. The coordinator Jörgen was unsure of what was going on when he was working on an office that was open. According to the coordinator Jörgen, they most often do not have to imprison the incumbents, though it happens. But not so often, the coordinator Jörgen refers to the prison law, so it will be correct. He said that now, with the new rules, a VB (Executive Commander) was required to

decide whether the detained person would have a detention or not. When, at one point, I talked with client handler Peter, he almost said the same thing as coordinator Jörgen. According to client Peter, it is usually the law enforcement to decide whether to imprison a detention, even if it usually happens in consultation with the affected doctor, I understand that.

When it comes to cheat prison, it is usually used only when metal handcuffs can not be used, for example when an intake is inserted into the X-ray or the like. Something else, client handler Peter could not imagine. So now, when I've seen the prosecution from the inside for a couples of years, I can only say the following. In the case of the above question, there is a detention of individual to individual. That is a decision of a VB according to current rules is required. Then my statement is following we have a regulatory framework without rules that a VB must assess. Is it legal certainty? As much here in life, it is a question of interpretation.

But back to my life story.

Chapter 15: Transport by air

When the transport arrived after four days, new routines became clear. The hours went fast now. So it was just to accompany, even though some energy was required. Then I was on my way to an office, there was something new that happened, all new stuff made me quite tired when I became brain-tired after a lot of new experiences. The guards of the detention was without education so they have no experience how to handle people who had a stroke. The transporter also have to ask a lots of questions. Some of those who came from transport had received cardiopulmonary rescue, so they could handle a person who had a cardiac arrest. However, not a person who had a stroke. They simply could not handle such a person. Do not think many within the prosecution can handle such persons. Probably, only healthcare professionals can handle them, such as nurses and doctors.

The transport staff helped me all the time so I had the opportunity to get to the bus I would go to. There were two men who helped me and gave me support. I entered the bus with the help of the transport guys, so I had to get settled, and the transport guys got to help me put on the seat belt. Everyone who has a stroke knows that it is quite difficult with the fine engine, so it became a challenge with the seat belt as said! At that time, I was quite hard taken by the stroke that I recently had. You may always feel sorry for yourself. However, I never did. Sure, I've had it a lot of times. This is a trip you as a reader can follow.

Probably, you as a reader will be affected in another way.
It will probably put an impression on you and give you a
new view of the judiciary.

Just a thought... I can see for myself how this trip affected
me. I'm obviously not the same peson when I came to
custody. Just sitting in a transport bus that was going to be
a cuckoo is just one fact I have to realize. Certainly it
hurts to realize that I am now on my way to earn a lot of
years on the pitcher. Probably hard to take as a reader,
and get the same feeling I had at this time. Anyone who
believes that I have hurt and injured them in the crimes
for which I am convicted is likely to see that I have received a punishment that I deserve and suffer from. So harm-
ful joy is the true joy. As a person, you are sometimes
quite revengeful or want some payback to feel good. You
can, as a person, do quite a bit to get this payback, which
always starts with a thought and quickly becomes a feeling.

Back to my life story!

So when you as a person have dealt with the hate feeling
you have against someone who made life so mad for one,
it's very hard to enjoy such a person. I now have the ful-
lest understanding of someone who really hates another
person. I started to realize that I had many years on my
coat before me. When we went on the bus for a while, it
was now time for the airplane. The transport guys helped
me once more, and now I got support to get into the plane.
It was quite a small plan. The walkways were really
narrow so it was hard to walk. The transport guys put me

next to the back, after all, just waiting for the plane to lift, and every time it's the worst when the plane lifts and lands in view of the pressure in the cabin. Because I had a stroke, I did not know the woman's penis if I had to fly because it could be directly inappropriate when I had a recent stroke. When the correctional inspector or the VB (Executive Commander) had talked with the affected doctor who gave me green light to fly, it was a fact that we were about to fly to the dock. The planet began to rise sharply and we started lifting the plane. Up in the air, the pressure in the ears was significantly better. Talked a little to the captain before we flew and wondered clearly if it had a negative effect on me when I had a stroke recently. The captain did not consider this as a problem considering the planet went so low. To me, it was important words that made me able to let go of this topic. We were now in the air and the journey took about 50 minutes before we landed. The transport guy on the side of the row had worked on the prison I would add, he said it was a good place and the food was great.

The transport guy thought the transport department was quieter than being a funeral guardian. We sat there and talked, and soon it was time to go down for landing. The captain had begun the landing, something I could hear of the engines that now started to slow down. The captain gives a little to the right and the landing was now a fact. The pressure in my ears started tense as you understand. Soon the plane was down and the captain began to slow down, which was now quite powerful and affected everyone in the plane. Then one of the transport guys helped me off with the belt. Could be hard to understand for a layman how bad it was to me. I had no balance at all, so the transport guys who had to lead me, were not so happy that they had a person who had a stroke on the plane. They did not have any training on people who had had strokes. So it became a very strange place. The transport guys did not know how to do it at all. The transport guys helped me out of the plane and into the bus, which would go to the prison. When I was going to get off, I had to divorce from a friend I had been arrested with. We said goodbye, and he jumped into the bus again to get rid of the place he was going to sit on. It was not without me feeling it was heavy with all the thoughts I have to deal with. Because I had no balance, two of the transport guys helped me into the CV (Central Guard). That would now enter me on the prison. The dining room was on the side of a CV so the bad guys thought I looked like I ´m drunk. Because I had a very bad balance, the transport guys were allowed to lead me to CV. So it was not that strange that the bad guys thought I was drunk.

Chapter 16: Shack (Institution)

Once in a Central Guard, it was kind of a lock system that was going to go through. Because the doors would not open, the first door had to be closed and locked first. Then you could open the next door. Inside a Central Guard, a metal detector was standing so that you did not pick up anything inappropriate in the prison. Then I had to meet the security coordinator on the prison. He told me about a year that he never thought it would work when he first saw me. He said I did not even have any balance, and he thought it would a lot of staff are required to make this work. He simply did not see that this would work unless I got a lot of help. VB'n (Executive Commander) was probably also involved. Nicky Security Coordinator did not know where he would get this staff. Evidently, it was not just me who had a lot of questions.

Now afterwards, it became a question for the whole prison. The question was probably more how they would solve this problem, because it had become a problem. Security Counselor Nicky told me that there were two guards who would enter me. They had to lead me into a room I had to wait in. They brought food and drink. The guard BJ asked if I could leave UP (urine sample), or would wait a while. I said, - I wanted to wait until I had eaten my food. It has its advantages to go on liquid-powered tablets, you do not have to wait so long before you can leave a few drops of urine. The guards came back after a while, as they were kind enough to leave the room in which they left the food. The guards BJ asked if I could leave an urine sample, there was no alternative for me ... so I said no! So the guard BJ said we could go and try out clothes in the meantime. It was a bit to go, and for me who did not have a balance to go, it became bad to go. The guard BJ helped me keep a balance and it did the guard Jenny too. Walking and walking in a staircase is by no means easy when it's balanced. I became so dependent on other people for my everyday life to work. Everything that's easy will be difficult. A small sketch was difficult to fix. I used to fix things myself and was now dependent on other peoples. How damn could it be? It was a frustration that really hit me. Then sitting on a shelf, where the coward's nose has a strong foothold, and gossip becomes the devil's radio, which I did not like at all was fun, but whats my choice? I had to start relying on people, which I had difficulty accepting. It was a human feeling I received that made me think so. I'm like someone who's hard to trust people. As you probably know, the thought quickly became a feeling, and I got a mental feeling to fight.

Now we were about to try out clothes in the store. Even though I had a feeling that, at least, was strange, it was just a feeling. Once in the clothing store, Jenny went out of the clothing store. She would show respect for someone who would try clothes. She was new at work, but she still had a little feeling of being inmates. I had to try a lot of sizes so the guys knew what color of the bag they would take, so I got the right starter. The guard BJ was friendly and carried the bag because my balance was not good. Now it was time for me to leave an UP (urine stample).

The guard BJ entered a room to leave. I would leave an UP in a mug before entering a department. I had to leave this UP. Then it went to the infirmary. I was too sick to be in a regular department.

Chapter 17: Sickness Department

After a while, I was at the hospital department. Thanks to Jenny and BJs help, I came to the infirmary. Inside the hospital department there were two cells. Another intake that was already in the infirmary, caused the isolation to break as I was in charge.

I had difficulty talking about the stroke I had, so it did not talk much. Simon, the other inmates to the infirmary, was a nice dot. He told the guards to bring in coffee, when the infirmary had a coffee maker, he was always friendly to put on the coffee several times a day. Probably, he saw that my balance was very bad, It was quite natural that Simon would know when I have the Stroke. So it became a natural topic. Simon's first question were, how could they send me to prison. Simon was quite upset how they could send me on the prison. My answer to Simon was that I did not get mercy, as my lawyer had sent. Simon was not impressed at all about their way of treating me. There were quite a lot of questions about Stroken, so I answered these questions as much as I could.

The day began to end, and it started to get dark. Simon started entering his cell, and I realized that I was going to sleep the first night on the prison! Soon the guard came to lock the cell and then the first day ended. The guard said goodnight and locked the cell, now I was alone in the cell. On the floor was the bag that the guard BJ brought with us from the store we were on. I sat down on the bed, which was just a mattress, blanket and pillow, I was probably taken by the situation that was reminded.

On the floor there was a gray bag that contained parts of my new life. The thoughts began to become apparent, and I had to deal with them thoughts. Even if I did not want to. Had some extra pillows from the guards because I had to lay high with my head at night. The respiratory function did not work well after a stroke. It depends, of course, on where the stroke was sitting. For my part, my balance, speech and fine motorism were adversely affected. I was very hard with most things. It became a frustration that plagued me all the time. Just that I would do the smallest sketches so I had to think so that it really worked. Leaned me back against the pillows in the bed and pulled the blanket against me. I began to think of all the stupid things I've had over the years. Probably you as a reader if I regret things I´ve done. Even if I did not want to. I was very hard with most things. It became a frustration that plagued me all the time. Some things I regret and I could easily do some things.

The night was long and there were many thoughts that came back in the head. Is it sometime that one's thoughts get paid attention is it at night. I had a lot of focus on all these negative thoughts. It's a good thing if you have a thought, foundation, on something that I consider is negative. I would like to have a suitable answer to my thoughts that appear in my mind. It became very difficult on these occasions. I could almost take on the frustration I felt. First of all, the stroke I had, which made me unable to move as I wanted. Then all the questions that appeared in my head, without I any good answers. It creates the frustration I have to live with. I'm quite hard to convey the feeling I had. You, who read understand for sure.

The thoughts came and went, the first night was over and I did not get any sleep. It was my first night on the prison, now only a few years left. It was about 45 minutes before the guards would unlock the cells. 6:45 AM every day the guards would unlock. At 6:45 PM, the guards would lock the cells. In the morning, the guards said good morning, and good night when they locked the cells.

Everything on the prison was dramatically boring. I could almost stand the clock after the guards. It began to be heard scarcely from the cell door. - Good morning Persson, do I hear a guard say to me? It is meant to answer good morning. Only the noise was plentiful. The guards had opened the cell, and a new day on the prison was a fact. I thought it was hard to sit all day long. Now I was in the infirmary, so the mandatory employment obligation was not affecting those in the ward. They would have been a bit better if I had something to do on the days. The days became quite long when you have nothing to do. It will be a little talk with the other one taken in the other cell on the side. Coffee and food were the highlights of the prisonlife. Imagine looking forward to the different meals ... Talk about small demands on life. I had to get used to this locked and cramped life. I can not directly say that my new life appealed to me positively. There were a lots of new routines that I have to learn. So the first few days rolled. Anyway, some routines went pretty well. The prison bought a chair so I could sit down when I showered so I did not fall then. When it came to my medicine, it was not on the prison. In the morning, VB (Executive Commander), Lina, confirmed that my medicine was not

at home, and that she would send a guard to the hospital
so that they received medication from the hospital until
the delivery had arrived at the infirmary on the prison.
VB Lina did not say much more. She left the infirmary,
locked up and left. At about 11 AM my medicine must be
taken, and it feel safe to take important medicine, I probably got some extra punches on the pump (heart) before
I got my medicine. At one point, VB Lina came to the
infirmary and told them at the hospital, saying it did not
play such a big role if you took your medicine later that
day. Just taking it the same day, it felt a bit better for me
to know. VB Lina was a person who usually only said
what her case consisted of, she "cold talk" not very much,
maybe hard to make an evaluation when I only met her
twice. VB Lina said what she would do, then she walked
out of the infirmary, locked the door and retracted the
drapery, which separated the corridor from the infirmary.

Chapter 18: Arrival call

As an intake, you are entitled to an arrival call that a guard sits and listen in a speaker, so no new crimes are made. Today I would have to make my arrival call, a guard came and picked me up and I would go again with my bad balance. It was about 5 meters from the infirmary to the room I would call in. For me, I could not walk and did not have the balance itself, it became difficult. The guard was kind enough to help me and then I got a little balance by keeping in the wall. When we got into the room, I was allowed to sit on a chair that the guard put forward in a appropriate way. Even though I only walked 5 meters, it felt like I jumped 100 meters. Stroke is constantly reminded. I had difficulty breathing because the breathing function did not always work. I forget to breathe and then I became breathless. You do not feel good at getting air. I should then sit down on a chair and rest and breathe more stable. It feels like breathing through a straw. I look at the guard who understood that I needed to get the air before I could call my arrival call. After a couple of minutes, he asked if I wanted to call now if it felt good?
-Yes, I'm fine, I answered! The guard is called the teacher who is a good person. The teacher is a woman who is an older puma.

Anyway!

Meanwhile, as the teacher master fixed the phone, I looked through the window. Behind the teacher in the window, I could see ordinary people walking on the walkway outside.

I thought it was good to see ordinary people pass by ... maybe hard to understand for you reading. Even though it was the easiest thing in the world, I got new impressions. The teacher had received answers from my dear and my own children, Tobias and Alexander, knew now where their dad was. I thought it felt good to be able to communicate, even though I'm in prison. My own children now had an address so they could write letters to their dad. I'm quite empathy loose as a person and having trouble knowing what other people in my environment are experiencing or feeling. As for my children, my feelings became completely different ... I has very difficult to talk to my children in a cold way, they are my children who do not want a criminal father, as they have demonstrably. Just making an arrival call feels stupid. Because my children need a dad, not a dad sitting on the prison. You want to help your children in a good and positive way. I thank my children by sitting on a prison for many years. It's not without being ashamed of it. I hope my children will see that their dad is punished by their punishment and then will be a good dad who can help with the things a grandfather is expected to do. Anyway!

We went back to the infirmary after I had called my arrival call. The other inmate guy Simon was on his cell and rested when we returned after the arrival call. The teacher brought me to the nearest chair so I could sit down. Then she walked out of the infirmary and locked, and then she left. She was the contact person I would have but her vacation meant I would have another contact person for the week that came. The second captured boy Simon came out of his cell. Spontaneously, did he ask if it was good to call? Of course, I answered him that it went well.

Chapter 19: My own thoughts

There were a lot of questions that came up in my mind
about what I had done, and that I had not stopped when
time was available. There was a lot of thought that I
would handle and I sat many days in my own world, with
ignorant glance. Another day on the prison, and it started
to get dark outside. Soon a guard would lock the door to
the cell. The day was over and the night reminded me, but
a lot of questions I had no answer to. After the evening
meal, the time went quite fast, before a guard would lock
the cell. Another night was a fact. Should I sleep in the
night or would the questions bother me another night.
There was some night there was a lot of thoughts. I had to
be able to cope with this situation to get a wink in my
eyes. shit, now it was heavy. How could it be? It was not
without wondering why I did not do anything about it?
The question I asked was why I had not acted? Only after
I had myocardial infarction and stroke I responded. I
should do something when I saw that my own children
needed their daddy. Unfortunately, I did not do anything
about it at the same time. I love my children, so it feels
bad that I did not respond to the silent cries of their own
children on their dads. I have been a very bad father, who
has not been for my children. Probably it's quite easy to
tell you how to be like a person when sitting on the prison. To me, this prison life is a snap on my nose that made me react. To me it is a good father and grandfather,
more than on the paper. The morning started dawn. I was
quite tired, had sleeped quite late when all the thoughts I
had made it difficult to sleep. It was just trying to get into
the toilet. The stroke was reminded again.

As soon as I got up to sit on my bed I became very dizzy. Feels like when you get drunk and lay down in bed and close your eyes ... Then the whole world begins to spin so much that you have to put a foot down the floor. Just like that, you feel when you get up from the bed. Took me into the toilet and made me ready for the day. Just took me out of the toilet and put on my clothes before a guard came and opened the cell door and said good morning. Then there was a new day on the prison.

The question I asked myself was how I would get through this day. The days doesn`t start right away. Since I came to the prison on a Friday, it was weekend today. I came to the cell yesterday. So it was quite a few years that I would get through the prison. The weekends were heavy. What would you do? VB Lina worked that weekend. Probably no guard would work on the weekend. The reason I got it for me was why there was a lot of guard`s all the time with the food cart.

Chapter 20: The food cart

The fact that the food cart became a highlight of the day is a fact. Simon, the other one, always said to have coffee beans. They were an important thing for the day to go. The guard that came with the food cart asked if we want to have files and flakes, butter, bread etc. Simon was nice and took my tray because I had such a bad balance. If you do not have a fine motor, it will be difficult to spread butter on a sandwich. Type everything became difficult. Just eating their milk with flakes became difficult. Could have ask a guard, so I'd got help. But I was too proud to do that. That made me stop eating my milk with flakes. It was a matter of dealing with these sandwiches ... without butter, and that I had to eat those foods with physical problems. Everything became difficult. Just lifting a coffee mug without losing the mug became a full-time job. Simon often looked at how I would solve this. He usually did not say anything. He looked the most with his eyes saying ... how should this go! To me there were many trials that affected me negatively. Every day there was some trial that I would be exposed to. There was no doubt that these trials took on me. It's not easy to get into my situation when you did not even experience it. How can I apply empathy from other people when I could not feel it at that time? I ate my breakfast and then I tried to get the day to go. After breakfast, Simon took my tray and put it in the corridor so the guard could pick it up.

I felt that the shower was in its place. Now it was easier said than done. The prison had not made a purchase on a shower chair. So the guard had to go for a suitable chair that can withstand water and put it in the shower.

There is a shower in the infirmary, so it was only for me to go there. Not at all easy with bad balance. Just getting into the shower room is hard. Then I had to sit on another chair and take off my clothes. After a long time, it`s time to take a shower. The other guy, Simon, shouted in and heard so that everything was fine and that I did not fall. It's quiet, I answered him. Taking a shower may take 10 minutes for a regular person. No wonder Simon called for an hour. It took more than an hour for me to take a shower and put on new clothes. All I would do took a lot of time for me. Time is something you've got a lot of on the prison so for that matter, it was not a disaster. It was just trying to get the time to go by the days.

The food cart arrived at 11.30 PM with lunch. It was the same routine it was when breakfast came. Simon was kind and took my tray so I did not have to go with it. Once again Simon asked for coffee beans for the guard. We had a few bags of coffee beans from the guard who were there with the food cart. Now, afterwards, I can tell you how the food cart works. May be good to know. Upon enrollment, the guard ask if I eat everything or do not tolerate certain things. When the list of things that concern you is done, it will be written into a computer. Probably then write a VB in these things that concern you. Then the responsible chef can take a look at the list of things that you can not tolerate or not eat. It requires a high level of competence, such as a VB, or a correctional inspector. This list writes the responsible chef, and hangs on a bulletin board so the other chefs can see it.

Once the food cart comes to the infirmary, each food tray
is adapted to the needs of the intake. May be good to
know for those who read this book. Because the prosecution is a completely closed world. Monday to Sunday, it
was the same routines. We had three meals a day, so there
was no shortage of food. I did almost the same thing
every day. It was not without disappointing after a few
days. In the hospital department I was a week's time. In
the morning when I was moving, guard´s came as to help
me move. So I did not have to carry anything myself. It
was only to realize that I should move today. Simon, who
was the second in hospital, was both happy and gloomy
about move. Simon became himself in the infirmary when
I was moving. He only had one week to demob so he was
convinced to manage himself in the meantime. There were many thoughts I had. About how it could move. Practi-
cal things I would like to do was go to the shower and if
the prison buy the shower chair. I wondered if my shower
chair would go in through the shower room door. Just
such a simple thing, like there was a hose in the shower,
because I sat down and showered. I thought of a lot of
things, things were not a normal person who would even
think so. The more I thought, the more things I came
across. Soon it knocked on my cell door and two guard`s
came into my cell to pick up my stuff. The guard said
they hoped it would work in a regular department. Otherwise, I had to move back to the infirmary. The guard`s
helped me with support so that I could go. Then I had to
hold my hand against a wall so my balance became better,
so I could entered the A department, we went straight to
the right. I would be in line 30. The guard opened the cell
so I could go inside. A guard would go through the things
that were on the cell. It was a deep plate and a plain plate.

There was a cutlery, which was made of plastic and a mug. There was also a thermos. All this I would see after it was. Then I would take responsibility for these things. Everything that broke down was I personally responsible for. Which means I even had to pay if a few things broke down. I had to acknowledge these things through my signature. When the guard`s received my signature on the paper they went out of the cell. I started looking around in the new cell that would be my home for a few years. There were almost new furniture in my cell. On the other hand, the view was not so good, only looking straight into a hill that was quite boring to see. Fortunately, I did not pack up so many things when I was moving. Then it would have moved two times and it would have been hard to do that. I was myself in my cell and it was almost new interior in my cell. It smelled almost new. Because my balance was so bad, it was hard to walk around in my cell. All cells look the same. There is a TV, bed, and toilet. Started packing up my stuff in the bag, which the guard BJ and Jenny had assigned me. Toothbrush, toothpaste, shaving cream and razors were what the prison was for. That was what was free of charge in the prosecution service. There was not much in the starter, because I had to take a few things every time I went to the shower in the infirmary. So it was good not to have so much to pack up.

Chapter 21: The laundry room

It also means that I need to wash my laundry. Washing can be quite simple when the machine does the job. Do not think I need to address my bad balance. To carry a laundry basket in one hand and hold his other hand in the wall so I could keep my balance ... was not that easy at all! One of the bad boys saw that it was difficult to go with the laundry basket. So the intake helped me to the laundry room. He helped me with everything so I started the washing machine. The washing machine took about an hour to wash. I talked a little with the one who helped me with the laundry. It was quite certain that he asked what happened to me. It was only to explain that I had a stroke and had a bleeding in the cerebellum. That affected my speech, balance and fine motor skills. Then after I told him, he wondered what the hell I was doing on prison? Yes, I wondered, I told him. The intake had some questions and some were difficult to answer. Not because I did not want to answer his questions. It became impossible to answer all his questions. My knowledge was very limited in this place. After we talked, we went out of the laundry room and he went out to the TV room that was for everyone taken. I myself went back on my cell and waited for my laundry to be transferred to the dryer. After about an hour, I started walking with the support oft he wall, so I could get to the laundry room. Maybe about 10 meters to the laundry room from my cell. As you understand, it felt like 100 meters to me. When I arrived at the laundry room, I would put my laundry in the tumble dryer that was on top of the washing machine. To me it was a bad challenge to throw my laundry in the tumble dryer. Even a walk then I could hold a hand on the dryer so that I could keep my balance so I could bend down. It was one of the bad guys that passed the laundry room. He saw that it was a big problem for me to fix the laundry on my own, he was kind to help me with my laundry. There was a guard past the laundry room and saw that I was helped with my laundry by one of the bad boys. The guard asked if I needed help, because we'd be happy to help you, Jesper, said the guard. No, it's fine, but thank you! I replied. That it was infected between the bad boys and the guard`s, that was quite obvious. To me, it was only a clear statement, and to see how much of this anger had rotted itself between the bad boys and the guard`s. Just to see the eyes of the one who helped me with the laundry, when the guard came to the laundry room, was quite clear that they did not have much to talk about. The guard walked away from the laundry room when I did not want any help. Me and the other intake spoke a little while i got help with the laundry. We had quite different opinions about life. To me it was quite rewarding to talk about things that we had so different views about. Valuations are an academic word in the school life. It requires a lot of patience when you´re many years in jail. I did not have so much patience and it was not my middle name right now. When I and the other intake had finished our talking, we went to different directions.

Chapter 22: Brain Fatigue & Weakness

Once again I went to my cell and had a little rest. I often get brain fatigue after my stroke. That stroke was the hallmark of my whole life. Not to say that it has severely restricted my life. Whatever it was, I fell asleep for a few hours and got some punishment. When I woke up after a couple of hours sleep, I lay in bed with open eyes. My body did not want to get out of bed, even if I wanted to. Lie the most and stared at the ceiling. Could not get me to do anything. I was so tired even though I slept for a few hours. The question was, how I could be so tired. I lay and looking around the cell and found that the door handle was round. For a regular person, it may mean something. It did it to me. When you have a stroke, you do not have much power. Just lifting a liter of milk becomes difficult. What then happend with a round handle on the door. I had to use both my hands to get my cell door, when the guards had not locked it. Just to notice that the door handle was round made me mentally tired. I sat on the side of the bed and waited until it stopped spinning in my head.

My doctor who had taken care of me since I had a stroke always said it was not dangerous with dizziness, it could be uncomfortable to feel so. I can say that I learned to live with this dizziness, after much about and though. I think today it's just annoying with dizziness that makes me feel difficult every day. To me it is no longer an unpleasant feeling. Only a frustration. Halved now on my bedside and looked at the desk that was there. Most to see when the dizziness would stop and see how many desks I had.

As long as it was spinning, it was more than a desk. I looked at the three desk cases that were on the desk. After a couple of minutes the dizziness decreased and I was able to get up with my bad balance. I was quite shaky on my legs. I asked myself how the could be. Do I must have a stroke before I react? Apparently!

Probably my laundry was dry now, and I started walking to the laundry room using the wall that gave me a little balance. On my way, I met another "bad boys" who asked if I wanted some help. It would be the laundry in the tumble dryer I told him! Of course he said, and went to the laundry room. When I arrived, he was already ready and had picked up my laundry from the tumble dryer. He asked where I lived? -On cell 33 I responded. He put my laundry basket in front of my cell door. So it was just for me to pull the basket on my cell. The prisoner who sat in my laundry basket said it was about an hour's walk soon. He also said he could help me with support so I could go. The intake came to my cell and told me that they who wanted to go for a walk were allowed to do that. It was the same place we used to go for a walk when you were in the infirmary.

Chapter 23: Walk & Description

The idea was that the guards would help me to walk around the promenade. It was so infected between the "bad boys" and the guards so I always got help from the "bad boy" to walk around when it was a walk. After walking, we went to the department. There was not so much to do in the department. Some of them admitted played at the soccer game, others threw darts. I myself walked around the wall to get the balance when I left. On each leg (the department) there were five chairs with table, and another table where there was a coffee machine and a kettle. Also an egg boiler was found. In each kitchen there were two windows and a valve so fresh air could come in. Then there was only a corridor as there were only cells in. Every evening at. 18:45 PM came the guard and said good night and locked the cell door. It meant that the day was over, which could be nice when you heard every day that was not going anywhere. The fun is that I have never met so many millionaires throughout my life. The question you asked was why these millions of millionaires sit on the prison? They could only use a lawyer who brought their action. It's funny that they do not even hire a lawyer, because they are innocent. However, you do not get tired when you do not. For me it became difficult to sleep when there was nothing to do. Many of the "bad boys" who had spent a while had difficulty sleeping. They would get sleep medicine by the doctor. Before they could get sleep medicine, they had to fill in a paper about their sleep habits for ten days. There were many who did not want to fill in the paper that the doctor would receive. Probably the prison knew about this problem and realized this problem and requested paper from an intake that would have sleeping pills. In fact, these sleeping pills would be used as a form of drugs. Then you did not even have time to fill a paper, so it was certainly classified as drug abuse. Not only that I had a stroke that made my everyday life difficult. Only the kitchen in its entirety had a rigorous safety. This prison had a security coordinator who was the type of chief over the security guards. A safety guard that I had a lot to do, is security guard Mattias.

Mattias was very tough on the rules that apply. For someone who does not know what a safety guard does one day, I'll tell you what a guard can do. During my time on the prison, say almost two years, I saw a lot of safety work. Probably, a security guard has or had more duties than I divide. The following gives a pretty good picture of what a security guard's everyday life consists of. A safety guard is a regular guard who has become a safety guard. Want to say significantly harder in terms of safety. They are apparently thinking about security. Just following their rules makes my everyday life difficult. A security guard, security coordinator or a VB is required to open an intake security cabinet, where it has its valuables. They also educated the other guards in combat or if an intake was drunk or messy for some reason. They also learned how to get a prisoner to lay down so that you could put on the handcuffs. Security Coordinator, Security Officer made sure that no other guard came into dependence on anyone taken. Some things were directly inappropriate.

Getting into a dependent position could be a direct security risk. Everyone, or most decisions, were taken in consultation with the intelligence department found on the prison. Probably it was an extensive job to get a person away from a department. There should be a good reason to be able to move one intake. Probably the security officer is dependent on what the intelligence department can confirm. In consultation with the guards that client administrators have to bring in the case, the Criminal Investigator (kvinsp) will get the final decision on what to apply. When we come to a VB (Executive Commander), these can be extremely difficult with the powers they have to make decisions. Even though it is temporary, a kvinsp listens more on a VB than a "bad boy", most often they get through their decisions. A "bad boy" has very low credibility and is convicted of a crime. He or she is then deprived of liberty. So the credibility of a "bad boy" is not that high. In addition to the Criminal Investigation Officer (KVC), the Criminal investigator (kvinsp) is the most responsible for the prison. To understand who is responsible, I will explain how it works.

Here the order is.
1. Criminal Investigation Officer (KVC)
2. Criminal Investigator (Kvinsp)
3. Executive Officer (VB)
4. Security Coordinator (Coordinator)
5. Security Counselor (Counselor)
6. Criminal Investigator (Guard)
7. Ladybug (Prospective)

The arrangements 3-4 can differ slightly from the prison to the prison. Sometimes a Security Coordinator has higher powers than a VB. One might think that one should be able to go to anyone in that list. Surely you could do it, but if you wanted to get a decision you had to wait for a guard to ask one VB, before a decision could be made. The guards and everyone else in the prosecution must always be very clear. It was as a wise person told me that there are many diagnoses on the prison, and often you have to give superfluous answers, so you do not get misunderstood. Another wise person said that no one in the prosecution wants to make mistakes. The above statement means that the "ladybugs" make it difficult to answer questions from an intake. Because as said! No one in the prosecution wants to make mistakes!

That the "ladybugs" could not answer when asked questions made the "bad boys" frustrating. It was a prisoner that would answer an issue, but just became more thoughtful and frustrated than they were before asking the question. It ended with the fact that all those who took in went to an experienced job with their questions. The chance to get a response from an experienced guard was much greater than if a prisoner had to go to a ladybug. A ladybug often replied that they would return to the question. Thus, a question without any kind of response. I'm really trying to give you as a reader a complete picture of how it's on the prison. In order for you to understand, you must think like a criminal person sitting on the prison and realize that you are detained. Since you received important information about how and who makes decisions, I think we can start the trip now ... Then we go!

Chapter 24: The journey

I start my journey with you in the morning when the guards open my cell door and say good morning. I would go and have breakfast in the dining room. All meals were taken in the dining room when sat down or up at the A-house. To get up, get ready, go to the dining room and have breakfast. I would first get into my sentry-box to take my medicine. All this would be done within 30 minutes. Maybe it might be a good time to get these things on. It works safely if you can go and balance. The question was who would help me? when most people are sleepy. So who would I ask for help. The guards that were in the sentry-box were the ladybugs. Because I came to my kitchen during the holiday season. So the ladybugs who were in the sentry-box did not know much. They had to ask an experienced guard. In the sentry-box, client manager Lundh, who turned out to be the right hand of the Criminal investigator, came in. Client manager Lundh knew how it would be with the medicine. For a ladybug may not dispense medicine to an prisoner. First, you need to receive a medical education before you can dispense medicine as a ladybug. I got the help of the guards to get my medicine so now it was just for me to get to the dining room so I got some food. Shit, now I felt stressful to be able to catch up with all the things I would do. Most of the people taken looked very tired, and most had gone from the dining room. Yes, I was not immediately fast, so most were already ready when I got there. The one who helped me to the dining room was waiting and waiting for me to eat, he did not want me to sit myself. I felt it was very pleasant that really saw that I needed help. When I ate it, it took back the things that the dish would have. We would go back to the department again and the admirer helped me again, so I could keep the balance. It was supposed that the guards would help me so that my day worked. The "bad boys" helped me all the time so the guards did not have a chance to help me. The fact that there was a bad relationship between the guards and inmates was easy to determine. Just to see and hear how much hate they had taken to the guard was a little worrying. It had created two different layers, called them and we. Anyway, we came back to the department. The intake followed me to my cell so I could put myself on the bedside. The intake went out of my cell. It was a relegation to work and school, so he had to go to the production manager who stood at the entrance to the department so that the patient could report or write a sick leave. If you did not get sick if you could not go to the workplace, it was noted as a refusal of employment. A refusal of work leads to a hearing and, in the worst casc, a warning. One warning could only be 4-6, then sent to the police in the area where you can get extra days. One of the "bad boy" had 6 warnings, and was allowed to sit 21 days longer than the penalty decision said. For my part, I had 10 days of introduction. During the 10 days I had to try out different workplaces.

Now it was only a small problem, that made me unable to get the introduction, something to get in these days. The prison did not think it was appropriate for me when I was in bad condition and that my balance was poor. Once again I suffered from the fact that the guards were not trained on the person who had a stroke. So I could not get the help that I was entitled to. To sit on his bedside and realize that I can not get the help I need for the guard to get the skills. That should not be something that I should be exposed to. All the others went down to sleep so they could go to employment they were awarded by responsible guard. It was for me to take the laundry out of the laundry basket. Unfortunately, it was all I had to do during the day. Taking up my laundry from a laundry basket is quite quick to do even for me, tried to fold my laundry so it looked good on the cell. For me, things have always been my order. I was soon ready to get dressed and I had no more to do on the whole day. I began to get into the corridor. It was only the cell door with the round handle I had to take me by. Curse that they would put a round handle on the cell door. It is so typical of the prosecution. That should be the cheapest purchase. When it doesn´t work for me, or other people who do not have power is not that important. Only that is the cheapest, the prosecution will be happy ... Anyway! I walked past the cell door with the round handle and got out of the hallway. A corridor with only cells in. At the bottom of the door, which adjoins the TV room. Our leg there was a small kitchenette. There was a fridge with freezer downstairs and a stove. It was a stove that did not work because the guards had cut the wire so no power was generated. What the reason was that the guards cut the power cord, probably a safety measure. In any case, there were milk, file, flakes, bread, butter and toppings that could be taken by everyone who sat in the department.

It was the chef who filled up as needed. There was a basket that the chef had brought to order as the chefs had done. There was a basket to pick up every day when we had dinner. The chef provided that basket with a piece of paper that was filled in on stuff that was needed to fill. I saw that all departments had the same things. As you probably understand, a chef had an important role to fulfill when none of the "bad boy" would be without coffee in the morning. All departments looked exactly the same. There was a steel door that shared TV rooms and the department you sat on. To the left when I entered my department there was a wooden trellis that shared the kitchen and hallway. In each corridor there was 1 shower left, then there were 5 cells. I was in cell 33 as said. It was painted in 2 colors, in white and in some gray shades. It was something that I did not think was nice, I remember.

Sitting on the prison is very boring, there are not so many highlights. One intake did not have much to look forward to. For most people, the food and when you walked were the only things to look forward to. Walking was very difficult for me, as my balance was so bad. It happened that I had to sit down a few days before learning how everything works. Simply in the meantime, I'm adapted into the prison. Adapted in Swedish means that the other people in prison will contact and form an idea of how I like to be a person. Adapted takes everything from one week to a month, depending on how you are perceived as the person of the other people. For my part it took a little more than a week and then I entered the outer edge of the inner circle.

Everything became significantly easier now that you entered the circuit. It had become afternoon and they recieved came back after the release. They came back after some had a mechanical workshop, others had been in school and read. You do not become a rocket scientist immediately to study at the school. One gets the time to go. After the bad boys returned to the department, we would have dinner.

One of the inmates was knocking on the cell door and asked if I wanted help at the dining room. Something I thanked. For a long time we arrived at the dining room and I could go to a table while it took my food on a tray. Then he came to the table I sat at. I used to wait to eat until it came to the table, with its food. I had now got a seat at a table that was mine. Getting a seat at a table might seem less important. Then it was not in the prison world. Everything on the prison works according to the status of a person. The higher the status you have, you can decide on some things on the prison. That I now have a place to sit on is to go in the right direction. I had to start from the start like all other people on the prison. There were unfortunately no shortcuts to take. The intake asked for a while if I wanted to take more food. There was nothing I wanted, I answered him. When the intake had eaten their food, we went back to avdelningen. Now it was kind of at 17:00 a day, so it was not easy at all to get the day to go. It will be a sluggish day as long as you're in a adaptation. None of those who intend to want or dare to hang out with a person who is being adapted. I got the help of it taken to my cell after we had eaten. It was a little weird situation that has now arisen. Almost all of the bad boys would stay on their edge as long as I would be adapted. However, it did not apply to the one who helped me every day. It was a little strange because I can tell you later that it was in the inner circle. For my part, it was just at teasing around the department so the day went by. I went out of my cell and took me out of my department.

Would like to give you as a reader a picture of what looked like the prison I put on. When I get out of my leg (department), the laundry room was on the right immediately. Straight forward, the sentry-box. There were usually two guards usually because they did not have "solitary work" for safety reasons. To the right of the playground there was 1st TV, 1st sofa and a few armchairs. There everyone could sit in and watch TV or play football games. To the right of the sofa there were two microwave ovens that the inmates could heat their food they bought in the kiosk every Tuesday. So before entering the department, there was a gym on the right and upstairs to the short-term department upstairs. Upstairs everyone sat with short punishment, that is, all "short-term volunteers" also called coffee makers. As they often been called. The entire A house was at that time a short-term department. The VB and the guards placed everyone with short punishments on the A-house.

For my part who had a long time penalty, and then sitting at the B house, sat on the A house until I was in better condition and could start walking the stairs myself. The whole B house was just going on stairs all day so the guards thought it was not good for me. It was probably a good decision they had taken. The days did not go so fast. It had just been weekend so it was a little hard to have the week to go. I personally are incredibly stubborn. To have a heart attack first and then Stroke do not pay for me to write down these lines. Stubborn as I was, I walked around at the department in snail speed. For each day that went, I became stronger and would like to test different things. The guards were not so happy about some things. They did not want me to hit me. Walking on stairs was not easy at all. I just felt I had to try stairs and try my balance, which was not so good at all. The bad boys helped me go, even though they were on duty. Meanwhile, I am being wound up. That my life on the prison was so bland was a lot because people did not know how it would be. They did not know what they would say or do.

Chapter 25: Adapted

How to do or say to someone who has not been adapted. It's not that easy for the bad boys. It was clear they wanted to help me, the question was just how the bad boys would do? Most people want to help. You as a reader should know that it's not easy to just help another person on the prison. As a person, one has to think about his image. How would other interns appreciate you then ... As weak or? For me it was just getting the day to get stuck. I thought it was so dull with all the thoughts I had about sitting for many years on the prison. It was just working on something that had time to go, so you could have the week to go. I sat at the table inside the leg (department) that I was sitting on. The one who used to help me got past my department. I asked him if there was a chess game. He replied that he would hear if there was anything. He went away and came back after a while with a chess game he had found. Now it was only a small problem. He who picked up the chess game did not play. I myself did not have someone who wanted to sit at my table, as long as I did not get adapted. As a reader, you may think that it was a small problem when a person was not in the process of being ... You will see further how important it is to be adapted. I sat there with a chess game without having anyone to play with. I started setting up the pieces. Once it was clear, I sat there myself. Do not want any of the bad boys to get there and play. So for my part, just jump into my cell and wait for it to be evening. The evening came, and the guards came and locked my cell after they said good night. Another day had gone on the prison. There I sat in my solitude and did not know what I would do at all. It was early in the evening. The time was only 18:45 AM when the cell was locked. So there was a lot of thought during the evening that was very boring. I knew not what to do. It was taking the bed and watching TV, so the evening went. When I woke up in the morning, the chess game was untouched. There was no one who had played. Now only the chess game was set up a few hours after I went to my cell. The guards unlocked my cell at 6:45 PM every day. As an intake, you may only be locked on your cell for 12 hours unless otherwise. So another day on the prison was a fact that I would get through. Then it was a work Monday-Friday to which the intake should go. Otherwise, it will be a job refusal, and you do not want it. For my part, it became locked on his leg (department) during the days. It was a little sad to sit at his department all day when the others were taken on their job. Sitting on his leg (department) all day makes you passive as a person. Then you will read that the above daily routines I would have for many years to come. The duty of employment was mandatory. What to do if you were at the A-house if you had employment was to be in the workshop or at school. For some suitable people who had their safety level lowered by the prosecution, one could get their employment in the kitchen. Since the two guards that placed those inmates in the kitchen obviously had certain guidelines to follow if an intern would get their employment in the kitchen. The guard Milla was one of those responsible for placing in the kitchen. The guards was governed by the level of security imposed by the police. In order for you as a reader to understand, I will briefly try to explain this.

Chapter 26: ASI Investigation & Memory

Every year an ASI investigation will be done. Which sets the level of security that an intern should have. An ASI investigation goes on so that a guard or program leader puts a lot of questions that one should answer as an intern. The ASI investigation takes about 45 minutes to an hour. When the program leader or the guard asks all questions, the ASI investigation will be compiled before the prosecution can put your compilation. You are always yourself with the program leader during the investigation. Probably the result is sent to the region, then a security level is set for an internal. For my part, there was no alternative to going on a job. My health was too bad, because I would have a job. My balance was very bad, not to mention that I was often brain-tired and then I have to sleep, getting an employment means that I have to get it every day. For my part, there was no alternative to employment that I would go on every day. So it became for me to stay on my leg (department) and to be locked on everyday days through. Certainly, it was just about getting the days to roll. But what did I have for choice.

At the time I could not even write then my fine engine did not work at all. So writing my book was impossible, just then. It just became a lot of memory tags so I could remember what I would write later. My short-term memory was short and I mean shortly. I had to write down the names of the guards. Otherwise, just one guard would be a person the next day. I experienced it hard to fight for a small sketch, became my everyday life. So my bad memory made me write a piece of paper so I could not guess what a guard or what I bad boys called. Probably what my rescue to write my memorabilia, so I had something to do on the days.

Now it was about 1 hour to walk and then lunch so time went by. The intake helped me on the walk so I could walk around. When you reached the walk there were three benches left a few meters away. There was also a table there. Straight forward, a paved walk with a sharp slope down to the place who was a smoke area. There were a number of lighters locked on the safety net. If you wanted to get a cigg, you had to say his cell / room number, so the guards took a cigg from that box. We did not even have our own cig, even though the bad boys had paid them. I started to go for a walk with a helping hand. It´s took a lots of energy from me. I was tired after a few minutes so I was helped by the intake to go to my cell. I just had to sleep, I became braintiered by the walk. The intake would knock on my cell door when he entered, so I did not miss the food. The intaken knocked on my cell door after an hour after he was walking. Me and the intaken went to the dining room and the admiration helped as usual. I was so hard to imagine that my life would be so for many years. It was almost unreal that I would have to go through this hell. I got stuck in a system that apparently does not work at all. Me and everybody else in prison tried to make the day go. That was no easy task. Most of the people who were in prison wanted to go away from this place and many of them sang their vocal songs. Just to hear how bad they felt that the custody where they thought it was bad food on the prison. In fact, there were chefs who made sure we had good food every day. We were not in a res-taurant, but on a counter and would earn a penalty. For me who had stroke and myocardial infarction, it's hard to complain. Although I experienced that many days were hard, tough, not to say that you felt some things were very unfair. Not being adapted is one thing that affected me very much. I felt very hard, and even though I was not insulating, I was very isolated during the time that I was not in a hurry. The lunch was ready and we went back from the dining room. Half the day had gone and I would only get the other half to roll. We walked out of the dining room and came out into the corridor that was about 20 meters long. When we were in the department again, the guards sentry-box was directly to the left when we entered the department. The intaken was kind and followed me to my cell as he always did.

When I'm sitting at my desk, it knocks on my door. Two guards came to my cell and asked if I wanted to get a walker from the help center because someone from the prison could pick up one if I wanted to. I answered the guards that I would think of this and return to the question. When I talked to the intake who always helped me, it would not be possible for us to use the guards and help center to get a rollator. Pretty soon, the intaken walk from my cell. Honestly, I was pretty sure that it probably took a bit of anxiety because I talked to the guards. Although it was an important thing that would make my day work. I was not even embarrassed when this situation occurred. It was clear that I wondered how it had taken place in response to this situation. The question was just what he did right now, and how this would affect me personally. I could not go so fast, I was very addicted to it so I could get that much of the day. This situation could be a major problem. After about an hour, the intaken came back to my cell. Some of the interior had apparently found an old "cleaning trolley" that did not look much for the world. I felt I wanted to see the old cleaning trolley that the bad boys had found. When I arrived at the old cleaning trolley, I wondered if the bad boys was joking with me. Because it was probably the worst wagon I've seen in my whole life. It was in such a bad condition that it is difficult to describe. There were four wheels and one frame, then the rest was just crazy, on pure Swedish. The bad boys were completely convinced that some service and some color would make the noise. Personally, I was not directly convinced that some color could do the job.

The next day, the bad boys would take down the cleaning trolley at the mechanical workshop. Some of the intakes went to client manager Lundh who would approve that this cleaning car had to go down to the mechanical workshop. The client manager spoke with Correctional inspector who decided that the cleaning trolley had to go down to the mechanical workshop. The intaken helped me back to my cell so I could rest. It was not without wondering if the bad boys was joking with me. I had not been adapted, so there were a lot of things I was thinking about. Could be that the bad boys joked with me. Because there was a very bad cleaning trolley that barely clustered, so I was a little suspicious about this situation. At the same time, it was difficult to see that they were taking part in joke. The fact was that I would be adapted in, so it was not impossible for them to see how I reacted if a bad wagon came back from the mechanical workshop. I was a bit curious about how the result would be on this bad cleaning wagon. The one who always helped me did it every day so the days rolled quite well. It was the same thing every day, it was quite boring, but I had no choice.

There was a new guy on our leg (department) who played chess, so the days became a bit better. He had the same situation as I had, and he was also not adapted. So we had the same situation, so it became clear we were together. We played some chess games and then I went to my cell. When I was on my cell, I started taking new clothes, a towel and a shampoo because I wanted to go and take a shower. It would came a guard so I could go to the shower. The guard who came was called "Miss coldwater" because she would like to drive all showers like i did in a car wash ... she said it with the glimpse of the eye. For each time I wanted to shower, I had to go to the infirmary and then I was talking a little to this angry finnish ... I mean "Miss coldwater". No! she was very nice and there was a lot of word exchange. Because I had such a bad balance, I had to put a hand in the wall and my clothes in my other hand. Because I get tired quite easily, I had to sit down and rest. Now you should know that it was about 60-70 meters from my cell, to the infirmary I would go. To me it was incredibly far. Not only that. I would go as far back. I thought it was a long way to go. When I reached the hospital department and was going to take a shower, I was very tired. The guard "Miss Coldwater" got to go and picked up a chair that was waterproof. When I got a water resistant chair, just go. It was just sitting down on the chair so I could take off my clothes. Just getting rid of the socks was a full time job. Everything will be very difficult when I had no balance. For a normal person who is in balance, maybe 5-10 minutes of work. For me it took about an hour. Yes, everything was hard to do for me not least to go to the infirmary to take a shower that became a job for me thinking it becomes quite difficult to understand for a person who is not affected by this dizziness and the loss of the given balance. A balance as loose with my absence from me. It´s not because the guards cheated me, when I went to the shower. It was probably more that I felt an inner stress. Just going to the shower every day took about 7 hours a week. The guards had their salary for this. It was probably more my conscience that I actually took an hour a day, for a simple matter like shower. The guard "Miss Coldwater" never called me to hurry. By contrast, she could hear if everything was good, so I had not fallen. So did every guard. Even the "Teacher" I had a lot to do, which was also one of the guard that came with me when I went to the infirmary. When I was done in the shower, always the guard follow me back to the department. It was in the middle of the day and as usual, all doors were locked. So the guard that came with had to unlock all the doors. It was a bit for me to go. At first we had to go a little bit in a corridor, to the left, the staff department, to the right was a corridor, where there were two guest rooms to the left in the corridor, since a room belonging to the staff to the right lay a room in which the intervention force had its clothing and other equipment. At the bottom of that corridor was a hospital infirmary with a single cell and another shower. In the corridor I would go in, there was an office on the right that the VB (Executive Commander) was sitting in. Then there was a room to the left that the church used. Then there were a lot of small cabinets that the visitors would use. A metal detector on the right hand side, the CV (Central Guard), which was locked when it was taken in. The reason was that they could open the lock that leads out, which absolutely should not happen. That's why the door was always locked as soon as an intake came by. After the resume (central guard) there was a door that was locked. After that door, the nurse was sitting with a locked door to the right. To the left immediately there was a locked door then there was a staircase leading to the mechanical workshop, changing room and to school if you wanted to study. If we stay up there, there is another door on the left, leading to the B house, which I will return to later. To the right there was another metal detector that they would go through after they had been in the mechanical workshop or school at launch. Then there was another locked door, and to the right lay the dining room I ate in each day. A few meters further ahead of a locked door again. Then it was about 10 meters to the next locked door. After that door there was a gym on the right a staircase to the left that leads up to the short-term department of the A-house. Then there was a locked door, then I was in the infirmary down the A house. Since it was in the middle of the day and there was no release, my department was also locked. Want to say another door to. The guard "Miss Coldwater" helped me so I came to my cell, then she went from there. This exercise was there every day. It certainly does not sound so difficult for a normal person with a good balance. To me it was very difficult, not to say a sheer challenge to walk in these corridors almost every day.

Once inside my cell I began to put my laundry in the laundry basket. My towel was a little damp, I was allowed to hang in the toilet on a hook. When done, I would go to the department. There had been a new intake in our department. The Newly admittedly apparently after conversati-

on could play chess. Honestly I thought it felt good. Then
my day could roll a little easier. The first day that intaken
came to the department, just talking a little. Partly of what
it took for and how long he would earn a penalty. It turned out he had 3 months for drugs. He would be here on
the prison for 90 days. The intaken would land and pick
up his starter pack that the guards had given him. So when
we talk for about an hour, he went to his cell to pack up
and to get it done. I did not know what to do. I thought it
was hard to get the day to go. I stood looking in the
window in our room. There was not much to look at. It
was an angle building so you could see the department up
there. Then there was a hill I could see if I looked a little
to the right. Behind that hill stood a tall mast with a camera at the top. I looked straight there were a number of
fences with sharp barbed wire. At the front there was a
gravel road that used to be ordinary people. I thought it
was a tough feeling not to see what I wanted to look at.

As a person, you want to get new impressions every day
and not to see the same thing every day! I think it can be
hard to understand for you reading. You can try the same
thing for a week. Then you'll find it hard to look at the
same view after a month or a few years. You may have
easier to understand that a lot of things happen with a
person purely mentally to see uninterrupted views. I did
not think there was a problem at the start of the sentence.
It was enough after a month that I thought it was very
difficult. When I was tired of looking out the window, I
went back to my cell with the support of the wall. Inside
my cell, I began to think about how it was with the

cleaning trolley that Lundh's client manager gave green
light to renovate. It was really slow to get the day to go
because I had not been adapted to the department.

It took a lot of time to get a hole and the thoughts I had
for the moment did not solve my absence immediately.
That one can get so insulted if a person has nothing to do.
I was not an exception at all. Damn! It was sad to sit on
the prison and earn a long punishment. For me, it fell asleep, until those intaken came back to the department
from the release. Is something positive with stroke, so you
can sleep a lot. You often get brain tired. That is not good
at all. In the prison, brain fatigue means punishment.
After I slept for about 45 minutes, they were taken back
from the launch. They were back and the one who always
helped me to the dining room knocked on my door. I
shouted that they could open the door. Not a soul came in.
I shouted again, but even now it became the same result. I
myself had to jump to my door.

Chapter 27: The gift Hot Rod

When I opened my door there were five intaken that had done something they would give to me. Two of those intaken go aside, and there stood the old cleaning trolley which they had taken over. The intaken had welded brackets because I would put my coffee mug and also welded a holder for a soft drink bottle. They even had powder painted it in red color. It's really nice and they have taken a very good job. Not so strange that they admitted would show off their work as they had done. Even the so-called number plate with my initials where JP was on, The guys had welded on. Honestly, I expected big problems when I opened my door, and there stood five intaken. I know I thought I did not fall by myself. Probably the only thing I had to think. Then two of those intaken to the side went to show off the new cleaning car that they had renovated. The new cleaning trolley had also got a name that was "Hot Rod" which they had welded in. The fact that the bad boys had arranged this cleaning trolley meant that I was now adapted up in the entire department. So it became a good Friday, so the weekend could be good too. There was a lot of chess playing in the evening. Now there was a lots of people to playing chess with. Now that I was adapted. When I had "Hot Rod", my life became a bit easier and I was not dependent on anyone, because my day was going to roll as usual. After playing chess I went back to my cell. Now I had my "Hot Rod". Inside my cell, I had one more thing to do with. Every night my car was parked in my cell. "Hot Rod" was in place. I jumped to my bed with the support of the wall. For my part, watching TV fell so time went by. It was in the evening, and the guards came and said good night in the usual order before they locked the cell door. I tried to get to the toilet so I could brush my teeth and get ready for the evening. Then just try to get back to bed again. I watched some TV for an hour and then I was slumbering. I watched the clock and it was about 9:30 AM. So I sat down on the bedside and began to take off my clothes and crawl into the bed. It was another magic night on the prison to get through.

I slept all night and in the morning when I woke up, I saw some red that stood at my cell door. I had to put on my glasses because I could not see that far. I also had price glasses that shift, so you do not look twice. Having a stroke also means that you have a short-term memory like a goldfish. In this case I obviously wondered what the red that was in my cell was. When I got on my glasses I saw what it was. Clearly, thoughts and thoughts became clear when I realized that it was the wagon I received from those admitted. To me, it means a completely different opportunity to get myself out. So it was clear that there were a lot of thoughts I had on the various possibilities that were now a fact. I lay in my bed and thought quite a long time. It was only 20 minutes before the guards were to unlock my cell door, so now it took me to get me out of my bed and into the toilet, brush my teeth and get ready for the day. The guard unlocked my door at 6:45 PM in regular order. When the guard unlocked my cell door, they looked into the cell and said good morning. Then the guards closed the cell door.

Chapter 28: New Day

The day had begun! I could get up with the new wagon
that the intaken has done to me. I thought it felt a little
strange, I was used to be helped by the intaken to my cell
every day. Now I was by myself and would do most of
myself, probably it was a strange feeling that I felt. I
started opening my cell door with the round handle that
was just a challenge. Then I took out the "Hot Rod" which
they had received. Now I was in the corridor for the first
time with my new wagon and, above all, I was myself. All
those who were still in the infirmary were completely
silent and watched. The guards in the sentry-box did not
say so much either. I would go there and pick up my medicine as I did every morning before I went to the dining
room and ate my breakfast. On the way to the sentry-box,
one could see that client manager Lundh sat in his office.
She often had her office door open, so that probably the
air intake became better. Even client manager Lundh did
not say much. It was her eyes just saying that it was fun
that I could do better myself now. When I got into the
sentry-box and was going to get my medicine, the guards
thought it was fun that I could get myself and that they
were unwilling to see me go away myself on their own.
When I got help with my medicine, I went to the dining
room to have breakfast. Even the chef Monkan and
Sandowitch thought it was fun that I now got a wagon so I
could get myself up. I had to park my wagon and take
some support from the intake in order that I could get my

food and go to the table where I would sit. I had my seat at the table, which was now holy. One had to defend and earn his place at the table. I sat down at the table and started eating my breakfast consisting of two sandwiches with toppings and oatmeal grated. Then there was an intake that looked at my wagon and said it had become very nice. Probably it was an intake that saw that wagon before it was renovated. I said thank you for his positive attitude to my wagon. Then he went from there. Even the waiter thought my wagon had been good. I thought it was good that they liked the wagon, which for me fulfilled an important purpose. When I ate my breakfast, the next challenge started for me to put back my dishes to them in the kitchen. Luckily, the chef Monkan came and helped me with the things that would be back. I thanked her for the help and started the unlocking of the wheels mounted there as a safety measure, so the wagon would not start rolling from there.

I started to go to the exit in the dining room which was about 20 meters from the department I was sitting on. when I got out of the dining room with my wagon there were vowels on the floor I would go on, which means there were joints across the floor. The wheels on the wagon were hard, so there was a rather loud noise from the joints in the floor and the wheels on the wagon. It was so loud that the guards could hear when I came with my wagon. When I entered the department again, the guards I knew came to know. It was horribly loud from my wagon that rolled over the tiled floor that was there. Inside the departments then I had to get the newspaper for the day so

I had something to do on the day. Soon it was time to work and almost all the people gathered in front of the dining room so that they could cut them off from the workshop and school. Those who did not get there got a job refusal. Employment was compulsory, so there was not much to choose for the graves of the boys. They only had the opportunity to write a sick leave or to take a job refusal. In case of a work refusal, interrogation may lead to a warning. For my part, it became locked in my department during working hours. I had an introduction for ten days. Then the question was what I would do because I was very difficult with the balance. That was a problem that the two guards had in consultation with client manager Lundh. I started reading the newspaper I had taken in the TV room. In the middle of the TV room is a table. When I stood there, I could look into the sentry-box if I turned to the left, and turned to the right I could see the client manager Lundh's office so you know as reading gets a picture of what it looked like. I had a few days left for my introduction before I would get a job assigned. I tried to have the days to go. Because I'd be sitting on this prison for a long time, I would be fine if I had something to do about the days. At the time, I could not write my book. Then probably the time had gone faster. No! For me it was getting into my cell and trying to get the clothes I got from the guards. It was not easy at all with poor balance to stand up and put in a shirt on a shelf. I took a lot for granted, which just became crazy and a problem for me I take for granted that you as a person should be able to stand up. It did not work for me at all, as my balance is very bad. I began to realize that this would not work.

The question was how I would make it work. I sat down
on the bedside and really worked over this problem. I
thought well before I wanted to try my idea, purely prac-
tical. I started by putting all my clothes on the bed. Then I
began to fold all clothes I had, I got up and took support
and balance of my bed by putting my leg against the bed.
Then I began to put all my folded clothes on the desk, I
put my hand on the desk to get support from the chair that
stood at the desk, then I put my one leg to the shelf so I
could put my clothes nicely on the shelf. Unbelievable
what you can solve if you just want to. I was surprised
that I could solve it. I was also really tired because I easily get brain tired. So I had to lay down on the bed so I
could rest a little. My thoughts went to my clothes, not to
mention that I had put them in the shelf nicely. I actually
fell asleep for a couple of hours.

When I woke up again, there was food in the dining room.
It did not have to come any intaken to my cell door to
help me. I had my wagon (Hotrod) as the bad boys had
done, so now I could go to the dining room myself and
eat. However, I got help with the tray so the food came to
the table safely. As I said, I had my seat at a table. I sat
there every day and eat my food, all meals. It was
strongly felt that I had been invited to the department.
Everything became so much easier to do. I received the
help of all those who were taken and not by a certain person. Because even if I had my own wagon so I could get
up, I needed some times when I was going out on the
daily walk, which was for an hour every day before lunch.

Then it was not a good idea to go with a trolley. It was a walking tour that made it possible for you to go both on stairs and in a terrain that goes up and down. Having a wagon is not good at such times. I had to put my wagon (hot rod) at the door when you went to the promenade, two of the bad boys taking my arms on each side and began to lead me down to the smoke area. Down the smoking area there were two benches that stood like a L-form. Then there was a barbecue that we only had to grill chickensausage in the first year, and there were two benches that they intaken sat on and smoked. Behind these benches stood two guards, one of them get cigarettes to the intaken when they said what cell / room number they had. Then the guard picked up a cig in the box with cell / room number as it intaken stated. The other guards behind the fence had a security mission, probably the other guard also, but probably not active. The guard behind the fence never opened the door that was in the fence of pure safety. Outside the fence stood two more guards. One of the guards stood by the tree and stone which was at the walk and who´s gonna see what the intaken do on the walk. That guard and the guard who stood by the door as you walked out onto the promenade had clean guarding. I and the other people in attendance could only walk around in circular movements. As soon as you stopped or bent down to tie their shoes, the guards became very observant of what we intaken were doing. It was quite difficult to walk all the time, when I got tired so fast. At first it was only a lap, then I was so tired at the bad boys had led me up to my wagon so I could go to my cell and rest. I was so braintierd that I fell asleep for a while. Often I slept so long that they intaken knocked on my door so I would not miss the food. It was for me to quickly get to the dining room so I did not miss the meal. Even though I was sitting on the prison, I received a lot of help from those intaken. Do not really think I had received the help in the community that the bad boys did. It was an incredible help I received from them. I went back from the dining room after eating my food. I know I thought it was food all the time. Three times a day there was food in the dining room. It was hard bargain in the prison, but we got food in abundance.

Now I had my little walk with my wagon to the department, then it was locked in again during employment. It was the last day of the week and last day that I was locked in the department. At the weekend, there was no lock in. During the weekend all departments were open. So just walk around with my wagon. I got a training every day. But right now it was Friday and I was locked on my leg during employment. For me there was not much to do in the afternoon, so it was mostly for me to sleep. In fact, a brain is healing while you sleep, so it's good for me to sleep in a double sense. I both healed and got of sentence by sleep. It was good for me that I became brain tired so I could sleep. After I woke up that the guards had done their daily routines, I had difficulty sleeping again. For those who do not know what the daily routine is, I'll try to explain what it is. The guards did a daily routine every day as it is heard of the name. In a daily routine, a guard will look so everything works, lamps and similar things. They know different things so it's not loose. A guard must also ensure that the speaker system works by calling the guard that is sitting outside in the sentry-box. They'll see if the sound is good and they hear what the other guard says. Then the guard will enter the toilet and see if the lights are on, they should also flush the toilet so no drugs are hidden in the toilet. After that, the guard was ready with the daily routine. This routine made the guards every day seven days a week. The guards had different times every day, to carry out the daily routine. The reason that the guards performed this routine every day, for we intaken were not supposed to feel secure on the prison, when the guards came on their daily routine. As for the thorough routine, it was quite extensive on every routine there were always two guards. One of the guards had a backpack with camera equipment and other equipment that was good to have. If you were on your cell, a guard had to do a physical inspection before you could leave. Then you had to leave your cell so that the guard could begin the thorough inspection. Then the guards locked on the cell. Then the guard began to search through the entire cell. The camera had them to the ventilation and other areas that the guards could not see. There was a camera good to have. After the cell was searched, the guards also took the plastic bag in the trash if the intake had thrown something inappropriate there. If the guards were uncertain if there were any drugs, they could take it up with the security coordinator, or the VB who then took a drug dog. Both the VB and the Security Coordinator had a lot of powers, so a decision by these people weighed heavily. This could mean consequences for a person whom the guards thought had drugs. A drug dog marking a cell's cell was allowed to leave UP (Urine Test) directly.

Now it was not a thorough routine that made me wake up.
It was just a daily routine that was to be carried out.
Anyway, I couldn´t fall asleep for this daily routine. Good
luck, because it was only twenty minutes until we were
going to have dinner. I once again got away with my wagon which they intaken have done. For me, it was the
same routine for all meals. I gained support and balance
because they intaken were standing still so that I could
hold my hands on these shoulders so that my balance became stable.

Chapter 29: Help of the Bad Boys

The other intaken took my food to the table, so the food was on a stable seat. I had my wagon, but it was difficult to go with a wagon in the dining room when all the intaken went around there. For me, it was faster to put my wagon at the table I sat down and hit the "Hot Rods" brakes I had. I ate my food and went from there as usual. It was the same round again for me to go. Same boring clinker floor to go back with a lot of joints on. because the wheels on my wagon were so hard, it became a rather loud noise when these two met. In fact, the days and routines were quite similar every day. The weekends were hard to get through. It's a rather strange syndrome that you as a person feel that the weekends are so dry when sitting on the prison. That's exactly the opposite when you're out in society. Then you think the weekends are too short. It is strange that you feel so. Yes yes, I was back in the department after eating food in the dining room. The guards in the sentry-box heard that Persson was on his way back from the dining room. For me, just calm down when I returned to the department. Tomorrow it was weekend and I would for the first time experience a weekend at the department. So I was a little curious about how a weekend at the department was. It was undoubtedly a feeling that I wanted to experience in reality. That said, the department was open on weekends all day. It was less guards on the weekend and it thought many of the intaken were good. For my part, I've only had trouble with a guard once, but it resolved. To me it was a bit of chess so it could be evening. There were a lots of loss in the beginning I start playing. To me it was a good practice to just play. Clearly, I wanted to win, even though the profits sparked their absence. There was a lot of chess with them intaken. I was adapted, so it was quite easy to find players who wanted to play. We often sat in my department and played. We sat at the table I described earlier that was inside each department. To my left there was another table where a coffee maker and an egg machine stood. In front of me there was a trellis that was natural colors and then a corridor as there were five cells in. Then there was a shower in each department, as said. Behind me there were two windows and a valve. To the right of the windows there was a fridge with a freezer downstairs. To the right of fridge / freezer there was a sink and drainer. Above the sink there were two cabinets and under the sink two cabinets. So now you understand who reads what it looked like in the department. It looked like the other departments. To me there was not so much to do than to enter my cell after playing chess and waiting for the evening. It was only an hour for the guards to come and lock the cell, so the day was over. For many of the bad boys it was a highlight when the guards came and locked. I did not understand why they thought it was a highlight that the guards came and locked the cells. Obviously I was a little curious, why some people thought so. Now, afterwards, I can tell you that there were two reasons for this. Many of those intaken thought it was nice to be locked in their cell, because then they could be themselves. When the guards said good night and locked, these intaken lives began a whole different life. They could be themselves and as they usually be in freedom. These intakens are therefore unsure of themselves. They could relax from the prison when locking was a fact. Those who were really uncertain of themselves and the situation could cry to sleep throughout the night. We who sat down at the A house could hear them up there on the A-house upstairs. It was quite frustrating to have to hear when one of the time crook cried through the night. For us, who were sleeping down there on the A house, it was quite annoying not to be able to sleep because of the crying of this intake. What happens to such an intern, I will address later in the book. As for the second reason, why some intaken wanted the guards to lock the cell. In fact, it was an important wheel that made everything work in the normal order of the prison. Of course you wonder what happened, which I will explain to you. I just want you to get a complete picture of how it works on the prison. It's frustrating not to see the whole, but just get a few fragments of situations that have happened. First, I just want to finish by saying that I took my wagon and went to my cell and as you know, the guard would lock my cell. It was to watch TV and wait for the fatigue so I could sleep. Now it did not get much to sleep when the intaken was sad all night. I had to turn on the tv again because it was impossible for me to sleep. Finally, I had a few hours of sleep after the intakens Lamentation all night. I was quite tired and I was not less tired when I suffered from brain fatigue. In the morning I got ready and brushed my teeth. I was ready for another day on the prison. Because I was so tired, it was only five minutes before the guards would unlock my cell and say good morning. I started taking my wagon from my cell as

I always did. Today it was weekend and there was no breakfast. The intaken received only two meals. It became brunch at 10:00AM, which was supposed to be both breakfast and lunch, it would be a powerful breakfast that we thought would manage until 4:00 PM when it was dinner. The bad boys were ready at 9:50 AM at the locked door outside the sentry-box on the stairs and waited for the guard to open the door. The guards waited for the kitchen to call the sentry-box and say everything was ready. After that conversation, the guards opened the door that went to the dining room. It's a door before you got to the dining room. Most often the door was already opened, so we could enter the dining room. I do not honestly know why they bad boys had so hurry to the dining room. It was a long queue. Seeing them admitted that really ran there and those intaken the upstairs ran down the stairs. It looked like a cow-drop when everyone wanted to come and first get to the dining room. I myself took it very calmly. It was quite difficult to hurry when you have a wagon. Then you take it easy, so I saw it at all possible to stress. I was calm, and when I was at the dining room, it was not that long queue. I went straight to my table and the intaken was almost at the cook's front and was getting the food. The intaken always turned to me at the table if there was more than one chair to choose from. Then he was kind to bring my food. I used to wait to eat until the intaken came to the table. We ate our food, then he help me with the stuff that would be back. Meanwhile, as the intaken put the stuff back, then I unlocked the wheels on my wagon. For some reason, I turned around, I saw how two of the bad boys communicated by saying some cryptic words followed by a look that said more than a thousand words. Those intaken saw that I looked at them. So they stopped talking to each other, they just started going out of the dining room. I was awaiting the one who helped me to finish, he had begun talking to one of the chiefs. They had something to discuss that took its time. I did not want to pick up what I saw with the one who helped me. Because there may not be anything. I thought it seemed strange. I resonated with myself in silence. Unfortunately, this reasoning did not give any answer. Without a doubt, it was an issue I was thinking about. I'll be back soon at the infirmary. Obviously, it was an issue that involved me. I did not even notice the noise that occurred when I drove the wagon over the joints in the tile floor. I had to leave that question so I could think as usual. It was, as I said, weekend, so there was not much to do. You may spend time when you are new to the infirmary. I had new impressions that I had to think about. When you've been to a infirmary for a while, there's no new impression. I had difficulty getting the weekend to go, even though I had new impressions to activate my brain. Then an intake came and asked if we were playing chess. It was both fun and I had time to go. I also had the important training I needed for the stroke I had. It's hard to keep track of all the thoughts you have. Partly, there are some calculations that one has to do. One should rather see what the opponent should do for the next move.

Chapter 30: Thoughts

Being able to handle a lot of thoughts for a person who had a stroke, is like throwing up a stick in the air and where each stick symbolizes a thought. I was very happy if I could handle a thought. Chess is a game that requires that one person can think many thoughts at a time. At the beginning of my punishment it was quite easy to beat me. The more I played, I became better at managing the thoughts I had. Although I became better at managing all the thoughts I had, I could not just focus on chess. To act as chairman of the Confederation Council means that the bad boys have confidence in one. The current chairman would relesed in two weeks and they inmates favor of voting for a new chairman. Clearly, it felt good that they inmates asked me if I wanted to stand up in the election. We were two men who stood up as candidates for the chairman. I went into my cell and wondered if I could add anything favor of voting for a new chairman. For me, I was trying to get my own life back. Even though I knew it would be difficult and that would mean a lot of training. I was completely obsessed with coming back to life, where I could do all things myself. Because it's quite a lot to take forgiven. The reality had happened to me and I had to realize the reality where only thoughts I had thought about, meanwhile I went back to my infirmary. When I was in the infirmary, there was not much to do. What was good was that, I was in lamentation. The bad boys knew they could trust at me now. As I said, there was not much to do about the days, although it usually felt sluggish about the days, so I had to work with something.

Some of the bad boys asked me if I wanted to stand up as chairman of the Confederation Council. For those who read and who do not know what the trust council is, I will try to explain what it is, a little short. The Confederation Council is the union's own trade union. The Confederation Council shall conduct the proceedings, etc.

In the morning when I woke up, I could determine that I was asleep with my clothes and that I was in prison. When I had gone to the toilet, switched clothes and was brushing my teeth, the thought came back to the chairman that they admitted that I would like to apply for. When I got ready for the day and went out of the toilet, the stroke was reminded. I had a very bad balance and I noticed that when I was going out of the toilet. I became very dizzy in my head who feels like when you get a blood pressure drop, which made my balance bad. When I got out of the toilet with my bad balance, the guards came and opened my cell for the day. Now it was still a day on the prison to get through. It was the same routine every day I would do, say go to the dining room, shower and play some chess. Then I was supposed to have it for a few years. Honestly, I was quite focused on the chairmanships. I did not know if I could add something that would be of benefit to the bad boys. I would do a good job if I was elected president. Even though I used much of my energy, focusing on a possible presidency, there were many things that made me lift my eyebrows, both once and twice. The current chairman had a lot of things to do. The question was what he did? What was I going to be candidates for? The questions were quite many. Answering these questions was not easy for me to answer. How could I apply for a post, which only symbolizes a lot of questions without answers.

I soon realized that the trust council did not consist of shopping in the kiosk and setting up a receipt as verifications. Although there were a lot of bins that contained a lot of receipt. Other parcels contained a lot of appeal to administrative law and JO. That the trust council was like a trade union for the bad boys was pretty much given. There was even an instruction book, what confidence should contain. So far I thought it seemed serious and thoughtful. As I said, only the day had begun and I would go to the sentry-box and get my medicine for the day. Then there was going to the dining room with my "Hot Rod" as it really was heard when I walked in the corridor across the joints.

Chapter 31: The dining room

I ate my sandwich and some days it was porridge, which I liked much. It became the same kind of breakfast every day. Why change something you like. As usual, backing up some things when eating their food, it was quite nice to talk a little with the chefs when I had eaten up. They were quite fun and nice, even though they worked on the prison. When I finished talking to them in the kitchen, I went back to the department. When I got back to my cell, I would talk to my contact person about what I would work with in the days. Robin, who was my first contact on the pitcher, had spoken with the guards who was responsible for placement which concerned work. Those guards thought that a cleaning job was relevant to me. They felt that my balance was so bad that I might be able to practice it if I cleaned. They had put a person on for cleaning because I was often tired. It might be hard to get it yourself. It was only the night to get through. For the morning the following day I would start working on cleaning. It seemed interesting to start work. I had a lot of thought about how it would be to start working. Not least, I wondered how my balance would be affected and if I would be brain fatique with all new impressions. The question was how it would be if I got tired. I was pretty sure I would be affected to start working. These were just the thoughts I had, and only to try it before I could pronounce myself. Almost every day the other was quite similar. I did not really like the brain fatigue I suffered, but unfortunately I could not do much to solve this problem.

The routines were quite similar and there were not so big changes between weekends and weekdays, they were obviously heavy to get through. I did almost the same thing every day. My contact person on the prison came into my cell and explained that the prison management wanted me to move. I would move to the long-term department when I got better and could walk on stairs. The prison management had put me at the A-house where there were no stairs. I was not immediately impressed to move, but what I had for choice. Had the prison management taken something like that? There was not much you could do about it and even less that a person could do about it. May cite client handler Lundh's statement. Quote:

That clients can decide when this is going to the restroom, otherwise, the prison management will decide what the clients should do. End quote.

So it really was, I had to move to the B-house. I found out this move on a Tuesday and there is a guard from the B-house on Friday that would pick up my stuff. Now I had a few days to pack my stuff, it was just like Tuesday and it was a few days to Friday. I had a thick mattress that belonged to my bed that would be moved to the B-house.

I, who recently became president of the Confederation Council and all the bad boys who came with their problems, will soon be with their chairman. Moving clients so easily was typically the prosecution, it was an authority that was total without empathy. I did not have much to resist when the prosecution received something. It was just to keep up with this trip without protest. I was going to move on Friday so it was a few days left for this Friday. On Friday it was a guard to move my stuff.

There was quite a lot to move, and most of what I had collected was in plastic bags. It was a female guard in uniform that would pick up my stuff. It looked quite heavy when she carried my stuff. Actually, I had my "Hot Rod" full of stuff that would come into my cell at the B-house. Normally you do not have to look at a new department before you get there but believe it or not, so the law enforcement or prison board made an exception and I really enjoyed watching before I moved so I knew if it could be on this department that consisted a lot of stairs, so I knew how it looked at this department before I moved there.

The boys at the A-house were not directly impressed that I would move to the B-house. So to me there were mixed feelings about this situation that I could not do anything about. When I entered the B-house, all the guys came and greeted. Obviously there was a completely different climate and one would deserve respect. Some of the bad boys walked around the department and showed me how everything worked. All the bad boys had their little box in the fridge and freezer where you could put their stuff from the store that you had bought. Under each wash a number was placed and there was to be put the mug belonging to the cell that came into being. Everything was in order. As I came to the B-house for a weekend, there were not many activities to work with, so it became quite sad. It would have been better if I had come to the B-house on a regular working day, then the workshop had been running. Now it became Sunday, and as Saturday, it was damn boring. The weekend was that I thought what I would do about the days, so-called everyday. The guards thought I could clean the department. It was clear that I could clean a little in the department, that was good for my balance. A balance that I obviously did not have so much of, and it was very very bad. I supported myself every day by holding my hand against the wall so I got some kind of balance. It was quite a long time to sit on both the prison and at the same time learn to go and keep the balance. I would take the job at the B-house, which I did. It was not so easy to walk around with the cleaning cloth or mop that was available because I had to hold a hand against the wall to keep the balance and not to fall. Sure, it was tough. I had this for a week and I can say cleaning, actually gives better balance though it's boring. For every day that went, every week that went, I actually became better.

To the B- house ...

Again, the bad boys, took care and were polite as you would do on the prison and when this was done it was quiet again. A silence that was a bit embarrassing, so I walked around as well as it was because I had to keep myself in something so I could go and maintain the bad balance that I had.

Chapter 32: The cell

When I got into my cell for the first time, it was a bit heavy, purely mental. Again, I thought I would have been here for many years, and I thought that was a pain. In the evening when the guard locked us in, I was quite tired. I just walked in and brushed my teeth, then I crept into my bed and slept all night. As I said, I slept all night, but then you should know that when the guards closed the door and locked the cell already at 18:45 in the evening, then you were quite tired. I was so tired, so I did not even put on the tv, I was without a doubt so tired that I have trouble remembering this day. The morning was a fact, the guards unlocked the cell at 06:45. It should not be more than 12 hours between locking and unlocking. In the morning I sat on the tv, it was weekend and saturday so it was not the mandatory duty obligation today. Then I could stay a bit longer in the bed than usual. In the weekends, it's a bit better breakfast, as I said. It was served at 09:00 on weekends, it would be until 16:00 when we had dinner. It was a breakfast that every bad boys would have. At the B-house we had two kitchens and there all the food saved to cook in the kitchen. The guards did not like us bad boys to take food for preparing the latter. At lunchtime on weekdays, the guards closed the doors to each individual department. Because, yes, I do not know, but probably it was a safety measure because there were too few guards during that time, and while I and the other bad boys were down at the metal workshop, it was less guards in the sentry-box. I used to go to sit and watch tv. There was a TV-room on each individual department. At the B-house there were four sections, and four large tvs of about 50 inches. One sofa and two armchairs in each section where we could sit and watch tv.

In the morning when they got up from their activities, the guards opened the door, every single door. In the morning on weekdays at 12:00, we had to go down to the public dining room and have lunch. All other meals we ate at the B-house department. When we had eaten or rather, when I had gone down to the dining room with all these stairs, and ate my food, that was the same show again. I would go back. It meant that two of the bad boys did take the Hot Rod and one had to help me down the stairs. He held out his arm so that I could put my hand on his arm as a balance and then the other hand I held on the stairs, so I walked one foot at a time down the stairs. As I came down the stairs, I walked out through a door, there stood a metal detector like those at the metal workshop went through when they came up from the metal workshop for lunch. When I got to the dining room I was quite tired. You get pretty tired as you walk through the days and move like a damn snail. The whole body spread out and did not want to. It would have been much easier to lay down and say, no, I do not want to. There was no alternative for me. Has always been stubborn, and a real bullhead. I would like things to work in my way, or else I'll get the fuck out of my mind. It was quite lucky I was so stubborn or I had not come so far in my rehabilitation as I did now.

Just a thought... I actually want to turn to some guards that were great! First, I want to say "Margareta Falkeye" you always made me feel better with your boring exercises. Example 1: Anyone who was going to write a place of residence could borrow a pencil from the guards ... but not I, nooo. Margareta Falkeye first thought I would do her exercises, then I could borrow a pen of Falkeye. Her share price was not quite good on such occasions. She always did that ... She was just too much! I do not want to go into the sentry-box sometimes! At those times, falkeye came as a bad heartburn, wondering if everything was okay. Falkeye was always so ... I can now say that you Falkeye is a big reason why I can go for myself and that my balance has become so good, so I can almost run from a GUARD ... Thank you, Falkeye for all your help!

The guard Cecilia, you became a TV-leader and I was among them first hit. And you actually did a good job. Thanks to you, I have pretty healthy thoughts. I really hope we never meet again at work, then you have failed overall. Thank you for all your help and values.

For other guards, I would like to give a greeting to the A-house and the B-house.

Back to my life story ... After the food we went up the stairs in the same way we had gone down. We arrived in a long corridor that contained two doors. When we got into the department, there was a laundry room, a billiard room with a dartboard. When I entered the department, then to the left was the client manager Åsa-Rosa office, which she was also called for. It was the big boss right hand, or even called the small-chief among the bad boys. They

would love to keep her in a good mood, because she became terrible, so it became quite safe denial, even with
the boss, because Åsa-Rosa said something to the boss, so
it was usually the case. Sure, women have power, it is
absolutely certain.

After the client-manager Åsa-Rosa's office on the left
side, the sentry-box was immediately there, and on the
right there was a lift that went down to the silver workshop. To the right again you came across to the other kitchen department, and the other department. There was a
small table, two sofas, and a little chess and some other
games. In the second room next to this sofa there was a
table of ping pong and some other. Most often, the bad
boys sat there and played poker, but we'll get into it later.
We return to this bleak story of the prosecution ...

We go back and look straight into the sentry-box, where
there are at least two guards around the clock. To the
right, you have a door post and on the right you go down
to the silver workshop. If you go to the department we
have another kitchen there on the left, and if you go straight there is also a table and two sofas that you could sit in.
That means there were two teams. Foreigners against
Swedes, unfortunately. However, so it was. Most of the
time we went to our kitchen on the left, sat at the round
table and looked out the window and saw ordinary people,
the civilization that was behind the walls and the eternal
prison, as it is in the field of detention completely closed
world. A world that makes you completely excited and
just thinking about the idea of coming out one day and
becoming part of society, or the corrupt society out there.
It is certainly hard on the prison, but it is certainly honest.
That's quite a lot more than you can say about the life of
the Smithlife. After I had looked and looked at the so-

called Smiths in the window, I often chose to re-enter my cell. I had a little hard to handle emotions and thoughts that I had to have been sitting in the prison for so many years. It's quite difficult to get into such a situation when you have not experienced it yourself. Sitting in detention centers means detention. Not like many others think it's a lot of punishment and just eating water and crusts, it's not. It's about having nothing, you have no computer, no internet or nothing at all. The only thing you have plenty of is time. Time in a lot. When you come to the prosecution, you become passive in some way, purely mentally. You still try to keep your nose over the water surface, but it's quite difficult. As I said, I chose to enter my cell, I got tired and I became quite often because I became brain-tired. It was some form of punishment, because at least I could sleep off part of the time that my punishment consisted of. Sure, some think it was a punishment, for my part it was a little more like a mere hell. I really hope that you who read these lines will put you in the situation where you can not move totally when you can not go where you do not have a balance where you have nothing more than a foolish interest in getting well and be able to go like a normal person with regular balance so you can do what you normally expect. There are such things you can not do when you've had Stroke. You can not go, you do not have a balance, as soon as you turn around, it turns out that you have a spare for a whole week where you can sleep on sofa and put down your foot, you know exactly what I mean, it feels like turning around when you have a stroke. I chose to get used to this dizziness, as a doctor told me, dizziness is not dangerous, but it's badly unpleasant, and so it is. One can learn to live with it, but it is pissed off unpleasant, but one can learn to live with it. Then it will be better the longer the time goes by. The more you get used to turning around, the less spin it in your head, and that made you feel like thinking and exercising every eternal day. The bad boys or rather, two of them came to my cell quite daily and asked if I wanted to work out at the gym.

Chapter 33: Training & Gym

There was a little difference between the A-house and the B-house, because at the B-house there was a gym that we could use every day. There was quite a lot. Because I had such a terribly bad balance, I had to learn to go very slowly on the walkway. The person who was in the training, he became like some kind of P.T (Personal Trainer), because he was behind me when I was going to go on my walkway so I could improve my balance. Now it was terribly slow, I think it went 2 km / h. It was so slow that you almost got heartburn. Anyway, this speed on the treadmill increased gradually after a few weeks. Finally, it went pretty fast, maybe 5-6 km / h, and that was pretty much for me secondly, I could let go of my hands and start commuting with my arms. There's nothing you can do when you've had a stroke. It's very hard to get into that situation. It was very difficult to both move and move your arms at the same time, because if you had strokes, signals from the brain to legs and feet and arms and those where the signals should go, they were not directly broadband speed. They went very slowly and it caused problems when doing this. What was the hardest thing was to go at the same time to check the pages, I had a lot of problems with it, usually it did not work at all. It just did not work. It ended that I was walking off the walkway after my feet just stopped. When I got tired I went off this walkway. I did some exercises with my P.T, to keep up my balance. I had a hospital ball I would try to hold. All this seems to be astonished easily, but it was not. I prac-

ticed almost every day, I almost said, then I was completely exhausted. I might train 20 minutes on a full day, but
it felt like 20 hours, because I was totally over. It certainly
gave results, the result was that I could practice a little
longer for each week, maybe just half a minute to a minute longer, but for each day it became a bit better. After I
had exercised, I went and showered. The unit had bought
a small chair for us who could not stand when we showered. It was actually a good chair, I could sit down so it did
not get so slippery. When you have a shampoo on the
floor it will be slippery. I walked down on the stairs, with
a guard ho helped me down so I could keep the balance.
Then I had to go in and shower on the so-called hospital
department, where I first came in. Then the guard picked
up the chair and then I got the chair in the shower, which
was estimated to be three meters wide and four meters
long, it was a rather big shower. All that I could shower in
the usual order. It felt good to be able to sit, and there was
a hose that you could hold so you did not have to look up
so that you were dizzy in your head. Put it right, just wipe
it up and take new clothes and then the guard came outside. When we were done he took the chair and then we
went to the department. Now it sounds like a 5 minute
job, maybe 45 minutes. I went really badly, I had no balance, and it took a really long time to shower. Anyway, it
took a long time, but it may decrease over time, but when
I started it took 45 minutes to 1 hour, at the end maybe it
took 15 minutes. When I got up at the department, just
come in and put their stuff on their cell and then go and
make their sandwiches or whatever it was until the night,
before the guards locked the cell. Then I had to go back to
the kitchen, make my sandwiches, and I have to say that,

and I say that only once, The bad boys who helped me, they were very nice, they were always very nice. They tried to help me with both coffee, sandwiches, everything. There was nothing to prove that there were any negative, bad people, on the contrary, it was really good people.

I know I was supposed to take ham as the prison wreck had a big barrel. One guy he was called Biggi, and he was really big. Now it's so when you have a stroke, you do not have a fine motorik, and Big wanted me to calm down at my own pace. Now it was just that it was 4-5 meters queue after me, which was quite stressful for my own part. But Biggi, who was 2 meters tall and equally wide, so he was really terribly big, he held up the dish with the meet and then he wanted me to take a fork with my right hand and take this pice of meet. Now it can be said that it did not go fast, it went very slowly, and when I just got a bit on the fork it fell off again. Biggi said, just take it easy, and I felt that the queue just got farther behind me. Then Biggi turns around and asks to the bad boys, is any-one stressed or? I do not know if that was his size, becau-se absolutely nobody was stressed. No, I could take it how quietly. Now it took nearly 20 minutes before I finished, and the queue was really rude long, but finally I got my sandwiches with toppings, cheese and fries, and then they got a little packed on them. It sounds very easy, but as I said it was very difficult. When I got it wrapped up, Big helped me in with the bar of my cell, because I had to hold my hand against the wall to maintain the balance that I had worked on. Now I was tired, so I became very un-tidy, but finally I came to my cell and Big had the sand wiches on the dish, he went into my cell, placed it on my desk. I thanked so terribly. A quarter later, when Biggi had gone, the guard came and said good night as they used to do, locked the door and then you were there. Got to put on the tv, eat some sandwiches and brush my teeth, then it was good night. For now I was very tired.

Chapter 34: Watch TV

I saw some TV in the evening when the guards had locked my door. I probably thought of a few different things. The first meeting call you get when you arrive at a prison, when you call their children where you sat so they knew where you were. I think it took more than I had imagined. Because when you sit there alone, looking at its bulletin board that is in this case, completely empty because I had moved from the A-house to the B-house, I would like to think about one's child. How can you explain to your children who are no longer children, but adults, that dad is sitting for the last time and that it's really the last time. It felt like I did not even want to start that sentence for my children. Now it was just a thought I had, but it took a lot of energy. I was watching TV, trying to dispel the thoughts that I had on my children and above all my grandchildren waiting for their grandfather. Grandfather who thanked them by sitting on the prison. I´m looking on TV for quite some time and I felt I was getting tired, it was time to brush my teeth and go to bed. Said and done, I did it. I went to bed and probably fell asleep quite quickly. I woke up quite early the next morning and I had new thoughts that I was thinking about. Once again, my children were in focus. I could not let them go. Anyway, I got up, washed myself and brushed my teeth and waited for some breakfast. But then it was weekend, it was Sunday, and I say that it was probably one of the boring Sundays I've been with throughout my life. It was absolutely nothing. The only difference between the A-house and the B-house was that the B-house was a motivation department for long-term doomed, that is with long sentences. Then we could bake on weekends. We got ingredients like flour, yeast or whatever we needed. Anyway, they baked and in the afternoon when they had baked we had coffee, muffins and other things. You can say afterwards that some of the bad boys were quite crazy, but not me, but I sat there and I was completely innocent as you know.

Anyway, it was estimated that we could take the number of muffins per man, which some did not really understand, or they could not count, for some took 5-6 muffins and hid a little in their cell which resulted in some of the bad boys became completely out of muffins, and I think afterwards it's not good. Because it only creates an unprecedented impression among the bad boys, and especially between foreign and Swedish citizens. In fact, if there were theft from both sides, both foreign and Swedish, there was really no difference about them from another country or from Sweden. Sadly it was because, as I said, some became totally without their muffins and could not even cuddle. When we had dinner in the afternoon, taken our coffee and muffins, there was not much you could do.

You could go on your leg (department) or you could go to your cell or you could sit in the TV room. Anyway, there was one sofa in there, two armchairs and a table, it could seat eight men on each leg. You could play cards or whatever they had at your request, there were different games, monopolies and the like, or maybe someone would play some music. The only thing you did not have to get in because it was a security center, were burned discs, but we had to take in regular discs if we had applied for it.

Some who were very happy in music had done it, and played their music. But now it was true that some were from another country, and it did not make sense, neither of us who sat on the leg understood what the song was about, because it sounded more that someone begged than sang in another language. I went on my leg like I was in the tv room for a little while, then I went to my cell and I wanted to start packing up from the move from the A-house to the B-house. Again there was a lot of bags inside my cell to be packed up. There was nothing that pulled directly because it was not really fun either for the part to do this work. I began to insert books and late blocks, pens and the like that should be on my desk. The strange thing is that we are considered dangerous to have any weapons or something like that, but we were allowed to hold pens.

Chapter 35: Cleaning the cell

I think it is very strange today, because you can do a lot with a pen. But anyway, everything in the kitchen was fixed, scissors and knives and so on, but when we got to the cell we had to have our own pens. Very odd. I noticed when I put my things on the desk that the person who had the cell before me had not been cleaned immediately. It was seen in the window, on the lists and in the wardrobes that there was a lot of dust, and then we should not talk about the toilet because it looked like someone had blown a hand grenade. Just pick up a pair of gloves in the sentry-box and then try to clean, using some chemicals we were allowed to have, but they were not corrosive, and if they had been, we would not have had them. I cleaned everything I could with my bad balance, and after a few hours the bathroom looked pretty good. I could start hanging up my towels and my necessities. Toothbrush, soap and the like. After the bathroom, I started wiping out the moldings, wardrobe, window frames and desk, a little around the bed that was stuck in the wall. Everything was concrete, everything was done. All glass was thick so that one could not accommodate. Armored glass sat everywhere. They probably thought we would run away, what do they really think about us? After I had cleaned, I started packing the other two bags with my clothes and hanging them in the closet so that it became quite inhabited. Then I was honestly quite tired. I had to lay on the bed that I had bedded. It took a lot to just get to the blanket. It seems very easy but if you do not have a balance then it's not easy to drop the wall and focus on stretching a blanket. It is very difficult. I'm pretty convinced that you understand what I mean. I actually spend the entire day and evening preparing for my cell. It seemed like hell. I would like to be happy, I would be there for quite some time, and the fact is than turning and turning it would be my home, not because I wanted, but because I had to. When you spend a long time watching things, you have a lot of time to think about things, and your children, and you have been a bad father, why my children could not call their father. There are lots of questions that come up in the head and especially when cleaning your cell. I would like my children to come but as the situation was now, it did not work. I continued my cleaning and tried to ignore my feelings that I had about my children, which I thought I had failed by sitting on the prison again. They would not have done anything just wanted to have their dad, and thanks for that I sat in prison. Not funny to say it but then it was.

In the morning, the guards came and opened. I had been so tired in the evening that I could barely brush my teeth. There was cleaning, hanging clothes, and preparing my cell so I would have a decent life. So sure I slept well. When the guards arrived in the morning, I had actually honestly just just got up. I was so tired so I was fainting. You get it and right now, I'm probably mentally tired too. Everything had probably come over me and I thought that, yes, now I was innocent but you had to sit on the prison anyway. Then people thought it was fun that the bad boy was sitting on the prison, and that one might think. But to me it was over me, I had come to under-stand, but everything that had happened, and especially the heart attack and the stroke which I had but made some difficulty adapting to the society and culture that existed in society. I could not even adapt to the prison because everything was based on being able to walk, you could talk, you could generally move. I could not do that.

Anyway, I had decided that I would manage this time. Which I did. The guards came as said and opened my cell there in the morning and a new day was a fact. A fact that I had to get out, meet my new friend and the bad boys at the B-house. It was again to be adapted. It's weird that you are adapted the A-house and then at the B-house, It feels like time has stood still. Now it was not really as I thought. I started to get out of my cell, so I had to stay the furthest wall. As I said, my balance is bad. I went out to the kitchen and outside the kitchen, all the bad boys sat and it became quite when I arrived. It was quite natural element because I was new to the department and everyone wanted to know who Persson was and what he was in for, yes you know everything. I had now come to what was called the long-term department. It was probably the most injured people you could find on this earth, I thought. It was we who had done serious crimes and had long prison sentences and had to sit in the prison for a very long time. So you did not reflect what you had done. When I went into the kitchen after I had greeted the bad boys, I went back to my place where I had my mug on the hook, would take some coffee, then it came to one of the bad boys and said he could pour the coffee because he saw that I could barely go. He poured coffee and then he put the mug on the table, I sat down and drank my coffee. He took his mug and he poured up coffee. He also began to talk about everything, weather and wind, as you do initially. It did not happen so much. We talked about the weather and then there came one more and soon there were 3-4 pieces sitting at the round table. Suddenly I was not in focus and it felt pretty good, even if it was so in the beginning. It would be a confidence meeting during the day, according to the bad boys said.

Chapter 36: Chairman of the Confederation

The chairman at the B-house had made his place available and now a new president would be elected. They knew that I had been the chairman of the A-house and wanted me to continue as chairman at the B-house, and if I would like to be elected if I applied for that role. Now there were a few things that made it so the question was why I would be. Yes, I did not have much experience with the B-house, I can not say that. When I had the A-house, I had a good reputation, and that's how you do in the prison, you get a trust choice by having a good reputation. After the lunch, we got into the kitchen. All the bad boys, the whole trust council came, including the chairman. As mentioned, the chairman opened the meeting and began to address the questions that were asked. Did you know what budget the Confederation Council had, what competitions would be during the weekend and what prices were allocated for what, then say that he made his place available as chairman. When the chairman had made it available, one would put a note in a box on the name that would appear to be the new chairman. Since I just got there I could not vote because I did not know what someone was called, and I did not know anything about anyone. Apparently people knew who I was, but it's always so, everyone knows the monkey, but the monkey does not know anyone. It was just time to wait and see what would happen to this. They had asked me before, if I could imagine sitting up as chairman, and then I thought why I could not do it, because I'm going to sit for so many years. Then it's better if you are elected as chairman so you can solve problems instead of hitting umbilical lint. When the vote was complete, the chairman took the box with all the patches and then put the secretary and went through all the pieces. There were only two names, another bad boy and mine. I did not really understand why my name appeared, but now, afterwards, I understand that it was based on being chairman of the A-house. You know everything with crime is like a big spider web, and as far as this presidency is concerned, it's a trust post, and it seems to be both good and bad. But in this case there was between 6-7 votes between me and the other Grab gravel, then I became elected as chairman of the Confederation Council. Which felt good. It ended with them picked me up as the new chairman. Everybody applauded, except me. I was probably more shocked. I was probably a little surprised, but now it was so that I had stopped and I had been chosen so now it was only to deal with any problems that would come, because they certainly came. The current chairman now handed over all the bids, all the verifications concerning the trusts to me as now the new chairman. There was also one elected new secretary in the Confederation Council that would help me as president so I did not have to do everything. Then a leisure liable was also chosen. When I received these, one of the bad boy helped me carry the binders to my cell. When we got into my cell, I put up my binders and it felt a little strange. I knew that this might be tough. I did not know exactly what I had agreed on but that trip you will join now.

The bad boy that helped me lift the binders in my cell went from there, and I started to look a bit in the binders, and I realized quite quickly that now there was another factory I had to do. Here was the order and reason, signed documents, minutes, receipts, verifications. Most often there were eco-robbers who were in the trust council. It was everything from lawyers, you name it, they were high, high officials, and yet put them on the prison. But I chose to read through, and then one could investigate one thing, there was an ongoing war between the guards and the inmates, that was, by itself, nothing new, but now it had apparently landed on a completely different level. One level that would mean that you were constantly on guard because it is this if you are elected to the Confederation Council, it is those who are first beaten (displaced) because they are considered to have so much control and power over them as others so that you are considered inappropriate on the prison, and if there were any problems, then the first ones were displaced, so it was chairman and secretary without any pardon. However, I just want to clarify what a trust council is so that everyone understands what it is. As mentioned above, the chairman of the Confederation Council has an overriding responsibility. He will keep track of what is available at the cashier through the treasurer, if there is a treasurer. They are quite synced. A secretary of the Confederation Council will help to assist the chairman in writing calls, posting posters, writing minutes for meetings, etc. A leisure liable is responsible for what it sounds like leisure time. That is, games, cards, baking, chess, pingis, whatever it is, landing it on the recreationist. Leisure managers may go to the chairman and hear if he makes any money at prices or the like. Or, in the confidence council, we save money for Christmas or Midsummer or something like that. It makes a trust council. That was the official plan. Now you will know the real plan, the unofficial. A chairman of the Confederation Council has the following obligations to ensure

that this works. A chairman of a long-term department
will look at them other chairman, that is, at the A-house.
They are directly subordinate to the chairman of the long-
term department. Everything that happens on the prison,
in and out, is responsible for the chairman. All money, all
tournaments and the like. Officially only official.
Unofficially, it's all about other things. If only we turn to
card games. There is a lot of money in card games, and in
this case we do not have cash and if you do not have cash
it's hard to pay. Then you solve it in another way. In this
case, you were solved with toothpicks. Toothpicks symbolized a certain amount of money. That money was
owed or you got the money. That money would be depo-
sited into an account, and that account owned someone
else. Because we did not have any other money, someone
else got to move it purely digitally in the world. This meant that they had to have calls, consent forms were sent
out, and some used accounts that others owned. In other
words, everyone else used the account that everyone else
owned to be able to carry out this matter. The problem
was just that those who sat a long time, some of them lost
quite a bit of money. Which meant they did not want to be
anymore, they would be moved, they would shoulder and
the like. The guards were on us all the time, and then I
mean all the time. You would like to know, they had
thorough inspection, and if you have thorough inspection,
I'll explain what it is.
A thorough inspection means that two guards go into your
cell, lock the door, empty the trash, take a small camera
and look at the ventilation, flip out the lists and erase
everything, and see them suspiciously, take them with it

and ask what is for something. You are thus held liable
for the situation. Depending on what the guards find or do
not find, I can only name a little fall. They found a notebook at one of the bad boys. The guard took the notebook
and there were only a lot of dashes. Certainly nothing
strange about it, but it seemed fun. The guards took him
questionably and asked what it meant for something. He
did not say anything, and they could not prove anything.
But they knew that there was some kind of game, and
they knew they symbolized money, but they could not
prove it and can they not prove it, so can they not spell or
give a warning. This war it was just one of hundreds of
wars that went on all the time. When we get to the cigg,
we had an hour's walk, which means they were allowed to
smoke for an hour of 24 hours, thus within 23 hours, and
what means 23 hours without a cigg. Yes, you do not ne-
cessarily need to be a rocket scientist to figure it out. It
will be a problem if people do not smoke for more than an
hour a day. This is obviously business, and business was
fine, but everything was still through the chairman, and
the chairman, yes, in this case, I was. It was a very weird
situation that became now, because suddenly one had to
control an entire society under the cheese cup. Because
that was exactly what it was. Inside the prison there was a
completely different climate, another society where we
took care of ourselves and where we were totally cut off
from the society that lived outside the prison. We would
take care of ourselves in here, and we did. We did it damn
well. It will cost and it will cost even more, but now we
have to join. Hope you're hanging out. I often became
brain-tired. There were so many tears to keep in mind,
many iron in the fire, and the bad boys clearly expected
their inaugural chairman to solve certain situations in one

way and another, and it had to be done because, as I said,
it was a matter of confidence. Now, then, I only mentio-

ned two things, card games and cigarettes. When we get to the cigarettes, it became problematic. People would obviously smoke, and even it became business, it became a good business. You could take quite a bit for a cig, 30-40 Swedish crowns for a cig, and that's quite the case, and you do not have it. Then it's like those who want ciggs, they will be guilty of money and get the money they have to make them send money. Then there is a so-called auditor. An auditor who does not exist, but still exists. This person who ensures that the money enters the accounts that the trust council can use in a good way. So everything hangs together, card games, cigarettes, everything that affected the activities within the prison, and everything would be a chairman with the main responsibility. He certainly had the help of the secretary, all around him, but, nevertheless, how to turn the ass it sits behind, and it was the chairman who had the main responsibility. Then you had responsibility for the second department, short-term department, so it became quite a lot to be done. Even the vouchers that came in, the receipt in the kiosk would be pasted, the budgeting, the treasurer would tell us what we had at the checkout etc. There was something all the time, so the time went by, the problem was just that I became so damn tired. I'm getting brain tired, and I had to sleep, and so often, it knew the bad boys. Cigg was something that went quite a bit and we sold quite a bit of cigg. The guards would like to look up all the cigg that came in, and they found only one tenth, barely it. But they found what they would find, and then there was always a joke, bingo, screaming them when they found a cig, but they just found what we wanted them to find. They did not find the real store, and probably they have not done it now either. When it comes to the money that would come in from the cig, and they did not come in. Well then, we had to, send someone who greeted the person in the cell who owed. Even that was a decision from higher words one can say. Often, it was a bit of turbulence and a little fights. There were socks of canned cans in, that's all we had. But it hurts to get a can of cans on your face. Then you usually pay. Many times, then, we had to fix it so that it became right from the start, as you probably understand.

I can tell you once again when nothing happened, but it was a rather funny incident. I was the chairman of the Confederation Council, the secretary who was trained, I can say, it was another guy who was not elected to the Confederation Council, he was about 2 meters long. We went to one of the bad boys who had not paid their bill, that is, we were three men, I was quite trained too. I had no view on my left eye so I had an eye patch over my eye. Then I was cut so I only had a small plate on my head. So you did not see that jeat out It was not the date you were on. When we came to the guy we noticed that he was walking against the wall, and I could barely walk so I always hold me in a railing or something so I could go.

When the guy sees that we are on his way, he walks against the wall opposite side from the cell, saying he should pay. We just want to talk to you, we said. We want to talk with you inside the cell. No, but I do not want to go in, he said. No, but we wanted to talk to him and we were quite convincing so I told him he got my word that we would not do him anything, nothing will happen to him at all. He entered his cell but he was terribly suspicious, he was nervous, you saw that. He began to stumble, sweat, he almost stumbled and then he just said I should pay, I'll pay. That's all he said. We just wanted to pay so that took 2-3 minutes, he the other guy stood at the door, I walked in and talked to the guy and the other, the secretary who was well-behaved stood just by the window and glided. That was enough. The guy paid the next weekday, then there was no more.

With that I would have said you did not want to visit their cell of trust council, and it was very rare people would not pay or could pay. Because they could not pay, they fixed money anyway. The money came into account, and it can be both positive and negative. It probably means that the person who paid his debt got another debt, and maybe that was not what it supposed to be when we were done we went out of the cell all three. The bad boy we had talked with he remained in his cell throughout the evening, he probably did not want to go out. He locked his cell from within. This means that you only close your door, you can not do much more. When we got out, we started talking three times and we quite agreed that that guy was quite nervous and he did not want any problems so we were quite convinced at the time that he would pay in one way or another and the fact is that he did. He will all be credited to that, he was clean, he became clean.

Chapter 37: Liquid funds

Generally speaking, a Criminal Investigator, has the purpose of making sure that the money comes in, that you can follow them. It is one of his duties to make sure there are no gaps. Now it is the case that there are gaps. So, the Criminal Investigator and his right hand, Client Handler, were always on us in the trust council of where the money came from, and it came in quite big sums. We did not get more than 3000-3500 a month, but still there was so much money every month. You may wonder where they came from, it was someone who gave them from above, not what I did. In any case, it is true that in this country it is true that they in the prosecution must prove that a crime has been committed or that the money comes from a crime, and it is not as easy as it is heard. For every time we got money, the Criminal Investigator wanted to know where they came from. We could only say charity, we could say what we wanted, the question is just what he could prove. Could he prove anything at all? No, usually not, and as a rule, only he could freeze the money, he could do. A few weeks, but he still has to commit crimes, and if he can not, he has to let go of the money and then the trust council will have access to this capital. It was not so smart to put all the money into the trust account because the Criminal Investigator had a much better view of this account. What then happened was to have any of the bad boys a debt or the like, so they sent the money to the client's account, where they could exchange capital with each other. Then the trust council did not have to be involved in the same way. Now you can wonder how he could keep track of all these accounts, and the fact is that

you can not, because this is the case in the area of the correctional, you only have one thing you can do. Either you
can write his name, social security number and an account
number, so the money is sent to the postgiro in the correctional, then it will be posted to the bad boys account. This
allows you to, send a number of money a month and then
it's time to stop. But if there are more than 30 men in a
house, it will be a lot of money. In any case, in the small
world of the prison. There are the right giant sums of money, plus there is money in the cash registers used for
shopping at the kiosk, tournaments and the like. A chairman of the Confederation Council must keep up with the
finances that you surely understand. But it's not that easy
when you have a Investigator in the ass trying to force
crimes For them, the money is from an uncertain source
or the like. You may think it's unclear because of this.
You can basically do anything to make sure you stop the
money, and certainly it may be temporary. But again, they
must prove it, and usually they can not. I'm not saying
they can not, but usually they can not. So now that you
have a little more information on how it can be done on
the prison, I want to tell you about my life and my story.
As you probably understand, the Confederation Council is
a kind of conversion tool between the guards and the bad
boys. Where the bad boys raise their questions on those
meetings that we have and which we will raise to Criminal Investigator and the Client Handler. Once a month,
the Confederation Council should have a meeting with
Investigator and the Client Administrator. I, as the chairman and the secretary of the Confederation Council,
would meet these two. We had to do that once a month,

where we started lifting the questions that bad boys had, and then the Investigator answered as much as he could or

returned them with answers if they needed to check it out. Now it was the short-term department, so there was quite a good turnover on these bad boys who were so short of punishment. So it was quite different between them in the B-house and the A-house. The B-house had more issues that were a bit more important, which would affect for a long time, yet it became the most crazy thing from the prosecution service. It was quite often then. They probably had totally misunderstood this with the meetings of the Confederation Council, because they took advantage of this situation that occurred once a month, and tried to get their message out because they did not think we bad boys, we had lots of things for us. Above all, the Investigator would know about the good mood of the department or the like. The Investigator raised the questions and felt a certain weight of these issues. Then when we were going to raise our questions, it was quite blaha, they wrote up the questions, but as said with a facit in hand, it just feels like it's looping. The questions just came over and there was nothing left by the prosecution service. No, it was so and there were many of the bad boys who had sat for a while saying that it was. We received our questions but we received no response, and we did not get any improvement. Because it's because you're locked up 24/7, you can understand that you have a lot of questions. They are coming all the time. That one with cigarettes or rather to smoke inside. It lifted up if we could have a smoke area or the like, but it was just like this could not be solved because there was too much fire hazard. Then we asked if we could have more time out, but it did not work either because there was not enough guards and there must be a certain amount of guards, because it is a security task so it could not be solved. Because when we were to go out or say the smokers, they had to go out and go for an hour on the track. Of which there were lighters that were locked on a fence, and on the other side of the fence there were two guards and handed out cigarettes. That is, we did not even have our own cigarettes even though we had bought them in the kiosk. You could buy cigarettes in the kiosk, but they were put in a box with the number you had on the cell. Then when they wanted to smoke, they went out and let them say their number on the cell, then the guards took a cigarette and gave to the bad boy that wanted. It may seem quite heavy and it actually was. It was really damn heavy riot. The fact is that when it comes to cigarettes, there was also a business out there. Because according to the guards, if you want someone else to have a cigarette from their box, you have to give their permission, and many times, if they had a debt to another person, they had to pay in cigarettes, and then they walked around and a cigarette, yes it is very worth the prison. Out in society it's not worth a dump but on the prison, it's. So then you had to approve that the other would get a cigarette, and then it was all the time. The guards would say that it was okay with a nick or something, so they could take out a cigarette. But again to the meeting with Investigator and the Client Handler.

That with the smoking was, as I said, a rather important issue, which we wanted to get out of the bad boys. Then they had another question, we would raise them up with that loop. There were internal programs that could be put on, such as yoga or the like. I do not think so much about that, it's probably more about having a better loop. A loop means that C.V (Central Guard) can put on a movie when someone wishes. Then there's a loop to all the TVs. Now we did not get it because it would cost too much and as Investigator said, the deal is too expensive and we can not decide it and it is centrally controlled from Norrköping. A town in Sweden.

As elected representatives, we chose to highlight the other questions. Even though, now, with a facit in hand, I understand that this was a pure shittalk by the correctional. They found a lots of things, and that's not good. It invokes people in total false security where they want us to lift the bad boys questions and then it will not be anymore. It's just about them to set aside by law, one hour a month to highlight our questions. More did not happen. So I do not even want to get into it, according to me, it was a clean shittalk for the correctional. That said, we highlighted the other questions and expected some kind of response, which we did not usually receive from the correctional service. After the meeting, we thanked each other and went away, more was not. As said, clean shittalk. After the evening, the so-called release from the activities, the bad boys would know what answers we had received from the correctional, Criminal Investigator and Client Handler. So it was a small meeting in the kitchen in the evening where we were told exactly what response we had received from the correctional service. Those like me did not get so much wiser, and we who are quite experienced in this prisonworld know that you do not learn to be either. After we had our meeting in the evening with the bad boys in the kitchen, I actually went back to my cell. Again, I was damn tired. It had been a meeting, a lot of information, and another meeting with the bad boys.

That's how it had taken on my powers. I realized quite quickly that I was not really fit for battle. I can not say that I was. Although I would not hurry my body, it just protested. It just did not work, and it may seem like some frustration. You want to but you can not and, above all, you can not work. So for my part, it was to sit on my cell and calm down and review the verifications from the kiosk, those letters we would make, those appeals we would make. As a rule, there was quite a lot of appeal, when the bad boys thought they had been violated and their rights had been violated. So they would be able to lift it up to their chairman who would in turn make letters to both the correctional and administrative law. I can say that after I had done the letters and, above all, read through certain cases, I was quite tired. Just went to the toilet and settled in. Then I actually went to bed, and it was before the guards arrived at 18:45. Then you can understand that I was very tired. I barely heard that they came in and said goodnight, had no idea about it, but apparently it was.

Chapter 38: Lock in the cell

They said goodnight then they locked the cell, and Persson slept like a little child all night long. When I woke up in the morning, and then I woke up that the guards unlocked my cell and said good morning, it felt like I had been sleeping for a quarter. I was still tired and maybe you can understand or you can not. Anyway, I had to go and get ready, take my boards, then go to have some breakfast. It differs quite radically between the A-house and the B-house, in the B-house we actually have own kitchen, where you make coffee and breakfast or whatever you want. As a chairman, you did not actually have to make breakfast, it was served when you arrived. Because I had a very bad balance, it was not immediately better in the morning when I had been awake and I went as a living ECG. I held myself against the wall with one hand to get out, although I thought it was a bit better with my balance. Or I was terribly optimistic. But it felt so. When I arrived at the kitchen, they came and poured the coffee and I had my breakfast, whatever you should have. It was someone who had cooked some food that they apparently had hidden from the guards so we could have breakfast. We have 5-6 people around the table. But it was quite good breakfast in the morning anyway. However, it's always someone who thinks that their case has been overridden and always someone who thinks that, no, the trust council could have done more, for me they could have written more, done something more, they could say something, they could protest, strike, anything. It is the power of a trust council, they can actually put in real resources if they really want.

Now, just the question, should it be, we should use our power and the instrument we are striking and killing a full prison. Probably then, it will be that the Investigator will make something called P50. P50 means locked on the cell. So done was no alternative. The question is, then whether to do something else that is smarter, maybe talking to Criminal Investigator or conducting any kind of dialogue or similarity, but the questions were many, and in fact, many of them sitting on the prison were not directly Einstein. Unfortunately, that was the case. Many times, it was those who thought their rights had been violated.

Yes, anyway, we ate our breakfast and there was a lot of food. Then we would go down to the work, and because I could not go, had a bad balance, I could not walk the stairs myself. Walking down to the silver factory was a rather long staircase. It was a very long stairway, and it would not be the Investigator I would go in. Even though I had to ride the elevator that was on the side with two guards, because I had a high security risk, and the security risk would not lower them because they thought I was crazy. Now I can not understand it, I'm very nice.

Anyway, I did not get it. This meant that I had to keep cleaning up at the infirmary, that was certainly good for me because it made my balance better. I had to do some trials, keep the balance with the broom, and it may sound very simple, but it is not. It's not easy to go with a broom and keep the balance. You take a lot for granted, you look at things, but you never think of it. You never think of the bad balance, you never think that it actually needs to signal a signal from the brain down to the feet. Then I did

not want it to be a snapband, it would rather be broadband. If it's not, then you win and get bad balance. On
weekdays when there was work time, each infirmary was
locked. This meant that when you cleaned it, you had to
call a bell, then it was a guard and opened a door, then
you had to go into the next door and then let them open it
and let it in there. Then you had to start cleaning there, so
it was all the time. It was so pissed out loud so it's impossible to describe. It's about basically that there was too
little guards right at that time. It could be anything from
going away on a matter, to an optician or the like. In fact,
this security prison that I put on meant that in principle,
they never had to ever say when to go or whether to leave
a clean security point of view. Before then, one could
hypothetically prepare an exemption or the like. So it
could be basically that you stood and cleaned and then
they came and said that, now is the time to go to the optician and we will go in 20 minutes. Then they ask if they
should wear civilians or uniforms. It does not matter if
you go with a guards who wears his uniform for the whole of the car, it is the case of the correctional service. Then
you can imagine that it does not matter if you go with
uniform or not. It is quite offensive to go with uniform but
it does not get any better because it is the correctional
agency's car. No, it does not matter whether it was uniform or not. However, I had to choose if I wanted ordinary clothes on me, and the fact is that it felt pretty much
better when you let go of the custody clothes. If only half
an hour then you had to bring your own clothes. It's quite
hard to understand for those who read, but when you get
there and get into the so-called real society, you want to
wear your own clothes, so it is. Then there was a lot of

handcuffs and belts on it. Everything was based on the level of safety, and we who sat there were, yes, less positive to life, you could say. They felt we were so untrustworthy that we had to have both handcuffs and belts. I might think it was a little excessive in my case when I could hardly go and barely had a balance. There were two guards who had to help me out to the car because I could not go, would I then accommodate or? Maybe steal their car? Yes, you know, sometimes it's really ridiculous. But again to the cleaning. For my part, I had two correctionals. The kitchen and the public space had kitchen managers. Then there were two correctionals and it was the same there. For my part, I was quite tired after I had been cleaned. Even though I said I wanted to go down to the silver factory, I could not do that because the Investigator did not want me to ride a lift. Now, I can not understand why the Investigator did not want me to go down to the silver factory. But considering that they were so careful before they moved me from the A-house short-term department and that I had to come and look at the B-house, there were those stairs, and then it was clear that the stairs down to the silverworks was too long. You should understand that I also needed to come down and get the so-called social workout. For it be sure that when you sat at the B-house, there was a motivation department and a motivation department, which means that you should learn to meet other people and spend time with them in a good and humane way. Equally pissed off, Criminal Investigator chooses to put me up on the top of the house, now I had a cleaning at the A-house as well. I had done what one calls the request, to go down to the silver factory and that I wanted to ride the lift with two guards. That would mean that with my Hot Rod and two guards inside the elevator that took about 15 seconds to go down with. But again, I did not get that because Investigator had decided that I was just too high safe. I chose to submit a request permit, and I wanted them to review the decision taken because I thought it was quite important that I had to go down to the silver workshop and meet other people.

Until my request was processed, I had to go back to my regular job as a cleaner. That was not good, but it was good for my balance. It was quite boring and it was difficult for me to adapt to the social bite because the only social life I had was to clean in the corridor and then myself, and then it is quite difficult to develop any social trend. When I had cleared the days, we all looked like a cleaner, sat down and some of us who played chess did it. It was actually really fun to play chess, it was quite challenging and you noticed that those who had a long time were really at play. They had nothing else to keep in mind than chess and all the rules that were in that game. I played and because I had a patch for my left eye, my opponents chose to attack from the left side where I did not see that much. It may be both positive and negative when playing chess because I saw nothing, but I got better and it was even my view. When I was going to remove the patch after a month, I had twenty millimeters of prism glass in the glasses. You can understand that it was like a clean frame bottle bottom. I actually chose to have a patch because I did not want such thick glasses. I know that the days are becoming quite bland, when I had a social life, the question was just how this should happen. You could have a social life without social intercourse, I could not even understand in my wildest imagination. How can correctional just think so? Is the prosecution thinking or just following a rule that is terribly square, yes, probably it is.

Chapter 39: The Regulations

They are following a very square rule, unfortunately. Anyway, one day, when we were playing chess, a guard said we had to enter the department because we were not allowed to play chess. This meant that if we wanted to play chess we had to do it in our department. True, when the other player you played against sat on another department, it was quite difficult to play. So already there, it was quite square, instead of letting us play chess and having that little moment talking to each other and getting out the so-called social network, even if the person was completely crazy, even more crazy than I was when I was most active. We had to go to our department because the guard had come and said. If we did not do that, it would only be a warning and then it would have been a questioning and you would not have been worried, I would not have done that anyway. So we shared on us and went into each department. I entered my cell, each department had 8 cells. I was of them 8. There was not much to do in the days before lunch was closed, and after the release of the silver workshop and school, the guards opened the doors between the departments. For my part, just passing the time until the release was a fact. When the bad boys came back from employment, we had a lots to discuss. Meanwhile, I had to do something constructively, I felt. It became so constructive that I watched Tv. I could not do a dew anymore. I sat in the big TV room at the department and started watching tv in the usual order. I had thought I would do something but I did not get that far and I did not get to much. Above all, I did not do what I had to do. As mentioned, the bad boys had quite a lot of them to high-light and one of the reasons I was chairman was that I wanted to get my cases done as quickly as possible. In this case, unfortunately, it did not happen, but I had to sit and watch TV and wait until the guards opened the doors, and when the bad boys came from the release, they came and said hi, just as usual. One might think that it is quite easy to go clean and be a cleaner. Yes Sure, it's easy, but once you get a little bit of balance, I've started to get, not much but at least a little, so this cleaning went quite fast. I had two departments that I would arrange and it could be done in 30-40 minutes. That means that the other 6 hours we had employment, I had paid for.

However, I did not know what to do. But again, I had them most of the time engage in those cases that would be lifted up to the prosecution, their headquarters and admi-nistrative right to get the time to go. When the bad boys had gotten out of employment we would go down to the dining room, as we had all our lunch downstairs in the dining room. All other meals we ate at the department. So it was the same routines that it used to be, up and down, eating, going back, so really it was quite devastating to sit on the prison. So terribly ignorant and sad and the fact is that those who say it's fun to sit on the prison they actual-ly lie because it's not. I came back after lunch in to our regular kitchen at the department. Obviously something had happened. The bad boys wanted us to talk. We sat down in the kitchen even though the guards ran around like yard hens and wanted to know what was going on. For now there was something going on. We had two camps between two different interns. They were of foreign character and Swedish, and it was very close that it would hit. As a chairman, you have a certain responsibility for both parties, regardless of whether you think so and the other, you do not think anything when you sit in confidence. We will be able to handle both sides, regardless of the matter. To me, it was more a matter of how I could solve this conflict without the one who was banging the other. Because I knew if that would happen, we would have guaranteed a P50. Guaranteed. Which would mean we are locked for at least 72 hours on our cell around the clock. Also means that those who smoke should not go out and smoke, and you can imagine how they will be after 72 hours. Now there were only two who disagreeed about a certain thing, as pissed off, if we were in the Confederation Council that had to resolve it and that would have to be resolved before the guard, the Criminal Investigator or the client handler lay in, and should they do it then lock. There was no alternative, nobody wanted it.

When we sat there and discussed, the client handler Åsa-Rosa came with a note, they obviously wanted a meeting with the trust council. What they did not go into. We only got a time as we would get there, and then we got to know what it was about. The other bad boys looked at me and Åsa-Rosa went from there. Everyone actually thought, including me, that something was going on between the bad boys. Somehow, maybe they could have known, but why had they already reacted, something had not happened. It was a very weird feeling. The question was just how to handle it, would you go inside saying that we already knew about it or would you just sit and listen to what the matter was about. Honestly, I did not know how to solve for the meeting with Criminal Investigator and Client Handler. It was quite difficult to prepare when I did not know what it was about, or rather, I thought I knew what it was about, but I really did. The secretary of the Confederation Council came into my cell which had also been called the client handler Åsa-Rosa. None of us knew what it was about or why we had been called. What was actually what had happened? Yes, you do not know. In fact we could not do that much, we could only wait 20 minutes ago we would be at the meeting, then we would find out what had happened and why Criminal Investigator had responded as he had done. What was going on? Why had the Investigator reacted so much and VB Lina and Andre? Yes, nobody knew, but it would turn out pretty soon.

We came to the office of the client handler Åsa-Rosa and the Investigator was there, we greeted them and then the Investigator began to tell us that one of the bad boys, or as he said the client, had a shirt down at the employment where they had made a shirt where there was muck and date when they were going to muck. Now that he came down, the shirt had disappeared and no-one knew where it was, and the personal did not know where they were. Then the Investigator pointed out that in the Confederation of Representatives we would raise the question and tell them that shirt has to arrive and as soon as possible. Both me and the secretary looked like live bird cages because we had not even heard of this problem. Obviously, there was someone or father probably at this time some of the bad boys who had bothered this shirt and got rid of it. The question was just who that was, and would this person acknowledge? Because there is one thing in the prosecution or on the prison, and that's never touching another bad boys stuff. You do not even go to the cell, you take nothing above all, and you do not destroy anything. It's an unscrupulous team, everyone who is sitting on the prison knows about it. Nevertheless, this would have happened.

The Criminal Investigator said that this shirt is comming back, if not it´s going to be punishment, and punishment will become collective and, by law, punishment will not be collective.

Chapter 40: Collective Punishment

But apparently, the correctional do not care about this. This would mean that if the shirt does not come out with muck and date, then the other interns in the B-house will not bake this weekend and will not get any ingredients from the kitchen. That means, one has hidden a shirt and the rest of us are being punished. Once again an illegal from the correctional. I and the secretary wondered if the Criminal Investigator or client handler anything else they wanted to pick up and they did not want to. So we had been called because they wanted us to solve a possible problem so that this shirt came up in one way or another. We went from there, thanking client handler Åsa-Rosa and the Investigator, and then we went out of her office and into the kitchen to talk to the other bad boys. There were only a few in the kitchen so we chose the secretary to make a call that we would have a confidence meeting tonight in the other kitchen, and then it became.

Meanwhile, I had to prepare this figure, and how I would angle this problem. For now, we faced a rather extensive problem, as one of the bad boys had done, but it became collective punishment by not ordering items from the kitchen for the baking next weekend. The evening came and all the bad boys came into the kitchen. We closed the door so that the guards could hear something, even though they were curious so they were fainting. I started by opening the meeting to say the correctional wanted us to pick up a shirt that someone has hid or done something else with. I described the shirt as a whole for the bad boys and then I concluded that if this shirt is not coming up, it will be collective punishment, and when I said collective punishment, it became a foolish life on the bad boys.

It was both the only and the other, and above all that they thought it was very illegal. Now, the meeting turned around so that suddenly the bad boys would know who the hell had hidden the shirt or got rid of it. But there was no one who would admit. One of the bad boys stood up and said, I'm shaking who it is, if you do not come up, I'll look up and kill you. Then suddenly, a man came forward and acknowledged. Then we had another bad problem. We had two alpha-males that went to each other. We ended up sharing them, and they were really cursed. Now I can not understand that he who had broken the shirt because it turned out that the person who had taken the shirt had cut it and hid it in the laundry, I do not really understand today what he was cursed about. Because then you do not, it is still an unwritten law. Equally pissed off were the very disturbed people who sat on the prison, they were not really healthy people. The guards were prepared to come if it did not get calmer in the kitchen and the VB came to see if more guards were needed on the turn. We got soaked down all the way, so the guards could stay away from our meeting. You are not sitting there if you are well or have not done a crime. The guy who had broken the shirt became quite lonely, it ended with he walk away, and now we had a really bad problem because if he goes from there on a trust meeting, that means someone will pick him up, and that's quite sure. Then it's just the question how to solve that situation. He entered his cell, he certainly sat at my department so he came and talked to me, even though he knew he was wrong. He said it had been so bad to him that he had written that way. He just wrote that he was going to muck, I said. Yes, but he had drawn a bull too, he said. A bull, I said. I do not want to be associated with a damn bull, he said. You mean you cut a shirt because the person wrote a bull and wrote muck and late date, I said. Yes, he said. Yes dear readers, you hear yourself. What to do. The problem was only that I had to solve this. The guy went into his cell, and then it was night and we were going to sleep. The thing that happens after locking is that the guards are moving him. Obviously, they thought it was too high risk that he remained on the prison so they had moved him to an isolation cell, then he moved to another prison to solve the situation. Thus, the situation that occurred had resolved itself. What was left was just that we had a torn shirt as we knew where it was, the question was only, would we get collective punishment or how would it be?

It was morning and the guards came and opened the door and said good morning, as usual. As a member of the Confederation Council, I had new problems I had to solve. The question was only once again, we had got collective punishment. Would not the bad boys get bake this weekend, even though we had found the shirt in a broken shape, we would still have found it. We had solved the problem. The question is just how the Criminal Investigator would react. Would he punish all of them because of one. Yes, you did not know that. Anyway, I heard 2-3 days after the bad boy that had broken the shirt that had got a move had been completely broken on the other prison. They felt he had become too freaky. He had that attitude and yet he sat on a security prison, but equally pissed off, he looked upward. This means that you get knocked and moved to another institution. Probably the bad boy had learned a homework. He had to go to the hospital after the treatment he had received. Sadly, I think, because it was not meant to end it for him.

Again, I had something to deal with, letters, everything, always there was something. It did not take long until we had the next problem. Some of the other bad boys had entered another department in another cell, snoring a number of doses of snuff from another person who lay in the cell and slept. Yes again, unruly law. You do not do that. In this case it was a foreign character that twisted 2 doses of snuff of a Swedish, but as it was now we had a problem again on the throat. The person who had stolen that snuff was not so welcome to the department. So even he was moved to the A-house, because he would soon muck in a month. So you can say that the guards regulated things quite quickly and that may be both good and bad. Many times, or often, it was pissed off badly. He did not get that way, there came two guards, asked him to retrieve his stuff and then transferred them with him to the A-house, he was allowed to live there in the meantime until he mucked for saying that he was not welcome at the B-house anymore. There might be a high risk that he would get a quarter in the air if he remained.

I went to the laundry room myself after I had done my daily chores. Actually, you did not have to wash during employment after you had paid. Did you know the guards well, that was no problem.

Chapter 41: During employment

You had to go washing in the meantime, in the middle of the day there were not many that washed. It was just us who were doing care. While I was standing there thinking, it's a lot of trouble all the time, it's always something somebody wants to do, or someone who exposes someone else to mass violence. Basically, the assault alarm went 2-3 times a day. If an assault alarm goes, it means someone gets jammed, so easy it is. So the guards had a lot to do. Then the securityguards always had to consider existing security. If the person is to remain in the department or get a mess, to maintain the security that is available. I started going out of the laundry and quite soon there was a loss of employment, it was lunch. Then it became the next thing, as I said, there was always something. Apparently it was really turbulent now. There were two of the bad boys who had gathered at the silver factory and now it was the real problem. The one of bad boys called the other fag and the other said nothing, he was less aggressive, and you must be happy about it. Anyway, you get out of employment and then you have to go through an arc, metal detector, so you do not bring any scissors or anything else of metal. We're coming out, we'll go for lunch pretty soon downstairs in the dining room. When we get back, it's quite turbulent, because the bad boy is quite annoyed to each other. He who was called fag does not go to his cell, the other goes in and beats him. He gets a blue eye, a broken rib. Now you can imagine that it will be quiet afterwards, but it did not. What's happening now is that probably we had someone called snitcher, a snitcher means that we have someone who joins the guards, and you do not have to. For a snitcher has no friend, it's simple. The guards are looking for them who has knuckles fight with or the like, but it does not lead to anything. This causes us to get a so-called P50. That's right, you heard a P50 right. I can say that it became quite infected because those who smoked cigarettes did not even have to go under a P50. This means that they can sit in their cell for 3 days without smoking. Certainly they can get patches, but as said, it became quite turbulent. The Criminal Investigator decides that we will get a P50 which means we can get into our cell and be locked up to 72 hours, which means that the VB will print a document stating that we are detained, locked up and we may sign it. So they have a lot to do. Then it begins what is called a interrogation. There was a hearing of 32 prisoners. Everyone was going to the Client Manager, and a secretary had documented everything. Now it was just a problem, nobody wanted to say anything. But 72 hours would go pretty bad, now we only had to sit 1.5 days ago and we were released from P50, thankfully. The hearings were completed and everyone was allowed to come out. You saw everyone who smoked, ran like a cows in exchange at the butter factory.

They just wanted to get out on the track and pick up cigarettes. If you do not smoke for 1.5 days then you get a bit dizzy in your head. You can not smoke more than 1-2 cigarettes after that, it will stop. Then they will not have to smoke anymore, so people were annoyed because of that. The question was only, we who sat in the Confederation Council wondered what had happened, and above all, if they had received any information about who had given the person the jaw because we had been concealed. As chairman, I went to the office of the client handler Åsa-Rosa and wanted to know if there had been any information about who had given up the person in question. As usual, she could not say anything and did not want to say anything. You had their privacy to think so that was a bit of a moment 22. We can not find out anything but we are all locked in the cell, and it may seem that it's not so dangerous to sit in the cell. But if you're a smoker, it's not so great to sit in the cell for 72 hours. Far from there. You get something called withdrawal, and it's not fun. Certainly, again, you can get patches, but it does not give that great effect. The client handler Åsa-Rosa probably had no information, or no one would have given her any information that was of decisive nature. It was that she was guessing pure Swedish. People were moved here and there, and it became really turbulent. If 3-4 people moved, it means that then the guards do not know. The question was more now after all these interrogations that had been with all people in all departments at the B-house, what the Criminal Investigator would do. Would return to the correctional service with the classical collective punishment that they used to rush on, or would they just give a blow to pure Swedish.

Chapter 42: Anti-corruption program

Yes, you did not know, you just knew that this was not so thoughtful with the law enforcement, it was quite square. Many times, I might wonder why they were doing this. They had their rules to follow, but the regulations were neither human or anything that would solve the problems of those who sat on the prison. As you surely understand, you who read these lines, is that the bad boys and guards had a little aggression to each other, and really it should not be so. On the contrary, it should be that we who need help and those who deserve a punishment should be able to get professional help. Now this help was more like a repository, a storage total without programs. Certainly, the correctional had some programs and I thought I'd read up for you which programs there were. In order for you as a reader to understand what an intake can receive for education while serving a sentence, I would like to inform you about the following. These are the correctionals training courses at the moment I served my punishment. On April 1, 2011, a new prison law and a new detention law will begin. This will be all those who are detained affected by. Courses you could get in the meantime, you earned your penalty.

Å.P - Relapse Prevention Special Discharge Action Enhanced Freedom Monitoring, ETS - Improving Thought Ability, ROS - Relations And Compliance, VPP - Violence Program Twelve-Step Program, Prism - Drug Program, Idap - A program for you who used threats and violence in close relationships, BSF - Behavioral conversation, Dare to Choose - Where You Who Has Abuse Problems Can Be Affected Under 25 Hits, One 2 one - An Affiliate Program Crime - Courses for those who want to stop crimes

These courses can be obtained from the correctional, the so-called program of influence in the meantime you is on duty and then a penalty is earned. So by the time I put there were these programs. There are certainly more today. I do not know, but I think so.

Again to the story of life on the prison ... As mentioned before, the client handler did not know much. We knew who it was, we in the Confederation Council, but nobody said anything. This resulted in the correctional responding by move people here and there. Yes, as you hear, there was a war as well. The guards were legally entitled to their side and we did not want to say a shit. This resulted in the correctional guessing and the result was because our people moved away from the department by them. So it was quite often, every week, every month. It was all year round. There were not so many positive days on the prison, or rather I did not experience that there were so many. When you sit in the trust council you have to deserve the place to be chosen. Certainly it may be quite honorable to sit there because, as you said, you are trusted in some way. Man for the bad boys speech, talks against the guards. We are, as I said, a conversion tool between the guards and the bad boys, as we can raise the questions bad boys wants to solve. When you sit there, you have quite good insight into the market that really exists. Again that with cigarettes. It may be card games. These can be drugs. This may be for recoveries. It can be about violence. For my part, it is true that when you come from the A-house they have a chairman up there. The chairman of the B-house is the one who controls the entire ship and the other chairman listens to it. This means that the person who chairs the B-house will receive much more demands. Everything that comes in, from drugs, stamps, tablets and so forth, I would not even have to do. I did not want to mix in this, even if I could. I have never ever thought of drugs, so for me it was so that I did not want to be involved. Equally pissed off, there were some parts that you were involved in. When you were in the A-house, we had no stove, we had nothing to warm up with. They had cut the power cord to the stove so that you could not heat up some things. As we said, we had a toaster to roast bread, we also had an egg cooker. The egg cooker was very symbolized for those who were wearing drugs. Because in an egg cooker there is a lot of water, most of them know, and in that you can put their tools. They were pretty picky, everything, just what would be there. There was a market that had the most. Some things you would not know how they had come in, you can only imagine. It was all from USB memories to porn movies, movies to the youngsters so they were a little quiet. The question is only, I know today how things came in. It's not funny to know, I have to admit. No matter which way it was. The drugs came in through women who had more holes than most had. The women popped out these tablets from their abdomen and then there was no more. They sold it on the black market on the prison. When there was a visit, you had to change clothes and then turn a lap so the guards could see that you did not get anything. Most often, they tapped tablets under the scrotum or similar to prevent them from finding them. Suspected them something in any department, then we went to UP (urine test). If we refused to make UP, it was quite simple, when you sat at the A-house, you could not be in the kitchen because you had denied UP. It was something all the time, as it was said, everything was from drugs, tablets, pillars, such as they say, to collections, and everything was supposed to be held by the chairman. It was not that easy every time because in the short-term department there were quite a few, and they were not just wise. Some were very smart and some were very wise. Equally pissed off, it became a crash sometimes, and now someone has to pick them down on earth, and we did, and that was what the guards knew. But they did nothing about it, or pretended to let them look between their fingers. Because it's like this, when a young boy came to the infirmary and was going to spring up, they were pretty quickly picked up, and that was what the guards knew about. There was nothing new to them. Even those who thought that they did not use violence but equally pissed off, I am totally convinced that they knew we used violence. There were very many good people, there were very bad people who just went as well and waited for their paycheck to come that was not suitable for that job. But it is well at all workplaces and this workplace was well, not an exception. As you pro-bably understand, it was not very easy to sit in the positi-on you did, and you noticed clay times about.

The guards, the Criminal Investigator, the client handler, and the VB, all went to the person responsible for the trust council, that is, the chairman and wanted me to talk with the bad boys. You may think it's quite fun for a while, but it's not that great fun. Because you know when it begins, for example, with card games, paying by toothpicks, you can realize that there is a lot of money and again people who felt mentally bad when they took on shoulder. I've been involved quite a lot on this round and I have seen and heard, even the chairman has emptied the cashier's cash register because of his game debts, and that's not good. The question is what you do, or can you do something about it. If you are in such a position, you should be honest with them, but there are actually many who handle it in another way and are dishonest by saying, empty the cashier and cover up their own game debts so that you do not get in bad days towards those other bad boys. At the B-house I was sitting on, it was quite notorious that if you wanted a move or a P50 you would have to sit at the B-house, because things were happening all the time, and the fact is true. The whole time there was P50 or it was a move, then it was the P50, it was always something and I can understand now that it was a rather tough environment that required quite tough decisions from the guards and, above all, from the Criminal Investigator. Because it is by law, it is their duty, the duty of the correctional to protect the individual while they earn their punishment, and this can be done in two ways. Either way you put your feet down or you are on sickness throughout their time, because you have the legal right to do that. However, there is no alternative when you have a long-term amount of weight because it will be quite boring. But anyway, there was a war between the guards and the bad boys. Yes, because it did not happen so much, you do not have to sit and talk about the same thing again.

Chapter 43: Knock (Move)

But I'll tell you about another thing. For some reason, one day when I was locked on the cell at 18:45, I got a bang. It knocked on my cell door and in there were 4 guards. I did not know what had happened and because I did not know what had happened, they moved me to the A-house again. I asked, what has happened? But as said, they had their orders, and I had to go over to the A-house. Guaranteed then we had a snitcher. For the day before, a small incident had happened. Yes, it was one of the bad boys who kicked the face of one of them old foxes, and that was not good. It made the old fox come to the trust council and said that if he does not calm down, it will get worse for him. More than he can imagine. Me and the secretary chose to talk to him on his cell, which we did. It was very easy to weigh and we told him what would happen if he did not calm down. He promised heed and conscience to settle down and after a quarter, I and the secretary could go away, and then the day passed just as it used to be nothing happened. It was not until, as said, at the lock-in as it knocked on my door. Had we got a snitcher, was it so bad? Was it someone who was just because of this or not. Why did they move me, or why did not they move me? Yes, I think later that it was due to two things, partly because we had been with the bad boys who had played the kung fu legend and that during the day I had the most of them sign a paper from the Confederation Council that they would have Some commitments made and on the paper they wrote, it was also a muck day. The Confederation Council wanted 50 Swedish crowns, and all those who agreed were to write that they deduct 50 Swedish crowns from the salary each time you received a salary. This ended with the signing of signatures and muckday. Muckday was because it would symbolize them to stop take money the day they muck, something else was absolutely not. I could not imagine that, but I could imagine that they were the two things I said before to get moved to the A-house. I went with 4 guards to the A-house and the bad boys inside my department heard that, now it became a damn life.

Apparently, they had taken me away, and if you had removed the chairman, it did not work well. They took my things, I took the most necessary thing I could take then I went to the A-house to install. It was a pretty bland cell, it was certainly in the same department I was sitting on when I got there the first time but on another cell. I had double mattresses, I got to bed again, and again I had to clean the whole cell because he who had lived there had totally forgotten to do it. When I was done with everything, all the stuff I had received, though, there were very few things so I would manage overnight. The rest would have a guard from the B-house come with the following day. I was quite hard to sleep, partly I was really pissed off, and I did not know exactly why I had been moved, nobody had informed me about this. So it became quite hard to sleep, probably I fell asleep on my bed for a while, with my clothes on, because it was not possible to crawl down and sleep as I should. I had no peace in my body, thoughts just went round in my head. All of the questions that would be lifted to the bad boys at the B-house were now completely impossible to do. The question was now only who would be the chairman, or who was fit to be a chairman. There were a lot of questions that were spinning in my head, but unfortunately I had no answer.

I fell asleep on the bed and next time I woke up, it was a guard that opened the cell and said good morning. Good morning, yes, you can say that was a modification of the truth. The morning it was good but hell, in me was not. Now I was back at the A-house, or the short-term department. Why did they put me here? I went to the sentry-box and picked up some stuff, necessities I needed. I was quite familiar with this facility, everyone knew what Persson was, unfortunately, and now I was back again. One knew the guards that were there, because there was some difference between the A-house guards and the B-house guards. Some would be on A and some would be at B, why do not I know, or I did not know for a while. I wrote on a request that I wanted to get my stuff. Wrote below and submitted it to a guard and then I went from there. I went to my cell again. I felt throughout my body that I was really pissed off now. At the same time, I had started an education at the B-house called One 2 one, I had gone 2 times and now I was angry. So I wanted to finish the education. The supervisor came and asked why and I explained why, and then she said that the only one you punish you is yourself and not the correctional, the correctional gets their money anyway. However, I did not think so. I was quite determined to quit, and then it was. She who was in One 2 one went back and finished my case. I myself walked into my cell and sat on my chair staring straight into nothing with bland eyes. I felt how to tremble inside, because you were so damn so you were breaking into molecules. But where did you help? One had encountered an anger and frustration, but as I said, it did not help me, it certainly did not help me. I sat there on my desk chair and looked into nothing when I decided to go back to the sentry-box and request them to confirm that I had been moved. The guard did not know nothing, probably beginner, and it was not good at all. There came a little more experienced lady with a little skin on his nose. An old guard that knew most about most, or at least a bit about the most. There would be paper during the day, the Criminal Investigator had probably sent over paper with them were not treated and then it was the Client Handler at the A-house who would do this. Then it would be placed in a compartment, after which I could ask them for a request. But as the case was now, I had to live in uncertainty and I did not like it. As I said, I could not do that much, I walked most around and wondered how to solve the case. There were some of the bad boys who wanted to play some chess with me and it was time to go. But the thoughts bubbled in my mind all the time, why had I been moved? When you wait for a response, time is slow, and I think that's bad. All day we went for lunch, dinner and supper, we were locked on the cell and the day after similar. I did not find out anything either. The third day when I went to the sentry-box and asked where my papers were, they had come, it was securityguard Mattias who took care of them. I was served to them and in the decision it was briefly summarized; I had been crushed because the institution believed that in order for them to maintain the security that was available, it was better to move. So that they could maintain the security that al-ready existed on the whole prison not only the depart-ment, and then one might wonder that it still was not why, no more than for any reason, that is, security. It may seem like a little yoke, but I sat on A-house.

Anyway, I can today, or I do not know if I can or want to understand it, but for me it's right that is right, and if something goes wrong, it's going to be correct. When you find out a message about a security symbol, you must know what points to break in order to break the safety. That's something I never knew, and that's what I can do today. I went back to my cell with my paper. Some paper had to be put on the cell and some were not allowed because of the safety routines they had.

Anyway, I was a long-term worker and would not seek permission only after a year and a half. It was quite a long time. I had both myocardial infarction and stroke so I thought it was quite inhumane I can understand that they liked the paper that existed and records that were there. For me it was very important to be able to get out and get more air for more than an hour a day so I decided to have time to go so I therefore appealed the decision to the correctional and the decision that the Placement Unit had said I could seek permission only after one and a half years. I did, I wrote this document, date and signed it. Submitted it to the client handler who would hand it over to the region. Then they had a week to handle the case. I went from the client handler after I left my appeal to her and tried to make the time go. I washed a bit, played a little chess, talked with the bad boys, went into my cell, so it was everyday. It was always other than fun. When I went there, thought so. Monday to Friday goes quite fast, because then you have employment but the weekends, yes, they are very boring. It happens absolutely nothing. On Sundays, it's pretty good because then it's bingo, and bingo may sound a bit old-fashioned, but we did not have much to do. We played bingo and the chosen chairman sat and weaved in the tombol and shouted the numbers, and all the bad boys there as profilent idiots and crossed the tiles. There were thus three prizes, first, second and third. Third was almost nothing, others were a little better and the first one was great. Did you get three rows on bingo then became the first prize, everyone wanted it so the weekend was saved. Now it was on a Sunday so really what was to save. Yes, have you sat on the prison so you know that Sunday is badly long so it's good to have some candy and other good so you could take out on time on Sunday. It did not happen much during the week, they had put me as a cleaner because I had been there before. I had two corridors to clean, it did not take more than 20 minutes. But the question is, what would I do then. What in the whole peace would I do more. It's quite devastating to sit on the prison because the time goes very slowly and when it goes very slowly, it became even more slow if you waited for something. In my case, I went and waited for a decision from the correctional, which I had filed for my permission. This would probably come on Friday, now it was monday and there was still a whole week left. So the days went on Monday, Tuesday, Wednesday, Thursday, that was okay. When Friday came, I went to the Client Handler at lunchtime and asked if my decision had come. Yes, that would have done, and I should be served. There it was said that the correctional had a rejection and found that the investment unit made a good decision. Yes, that means I'd be allowed to sit for a year and a half before I got permission, great fun. I asked the Client Handler if I could take my decision on my cell, which I received. I thanked me and I went from there. I was more annoyed than happy I have to say. As I said, I went into my cell, it did not work fast but I went there. I was quite determined to appeal the decision that the correctional had decided. If I did, they have 3 weeks to defend their title. 3 weeks. I wrote that I contested and appealed their decision and the intention was that they would send it to J.O, which they did not. 3 weeks had passed and no, the correctional did not change. Then I am entitled as a client to appeal to J.O. The decision that comes will then the correctional send to J.O and that was exactly when it happened. When those 3 weeks had passed, the prosecution would send it to J.O, now they did not do that. It was stamped an arrival stamp on it, the Client Handler and the Criminal Investigator had taken note of it and also the highest hens on the prison. I went in after 5 weeks to the Client Handler and asked where my decision was from J.O. She said she would check it out. Returns after lunch with mitt decision. When the Client Handler came back she was pretty pale. I'm called in her office, and asked again what my decision said, and that's when she said the correctional had not sent it. So I had and waited for 5 weeks for a decision by J.O that did not have J.O received. This is totally illegal and I would not accept it. It became quite turbulent, there were lots of letters here and there. The Client Handler apologized, even the Criminal Investigator came later in the afternoon and wanted to talk to me saying that it had been wrong and that they apologized so much and that this would not happen again. Everyone was now involved in my case. The correctional office, the Client Handler and the Criminal Investigator was involved. Evidently, the procedures had broken out. All of this happened behind

my back. It had become a major claim from the prosecution service. I did not notice this when I was sitting because it was behind my back. This resulted in them wearing a
number of weeks writing to J.O.

J.O read through and made a decision after a number of
weeks where they found that they were well worth critici-
zing for their mistakes. But where did it help me? I won
this case and I like it. It is nice to be able to win over the
Prison Officers. I like that sharply. But I did not get permission for it, I had to wait for my time as the Placement
Unit had said, and it may seem a little square. It only
shows that the correctional has a system that is totally
square and again where absolutely nobody wants to make
mistakes. The strange thing in this case was, indeed, that
most of the guards, the Criminal Investigators and Client
Handler all knew that the correctional had done wrong.
Yet they were loyal to their employers. Then I ask the
question why did them do that. They said something different between the lines but officially said nothing to
them at all. No, you can say I was not innocent, but I
earned my punishment for what I had done. I took my
time, but during the time I served my punishment, the
correctional did the crime itself.

However, they did not get any punishment. It only resulted in they changing the routines. Again, the higher you
sit, the easier you get away. The further down you sit ... it
becomes as if for me to be innocently convicted. No, seri-
ously, I was not innocently convicted. It is only true that
when you earn their punishment, you expect to receive the
assistance that you are entitled to. Not to be subjected to a
crime by an authority exercising punishment. It became a

bit strange, because an authority can not do anything illegal and at the same time get a right side on one of the bad boys, it seems very strange, very strange. I noticed, in my own mood, that I had been influenced by the decision that came from the correctional and that the correctional had apparently not sent my case to J.O. It made me feel quite easy-minded as a person, and you're sitting on the prison and having a bad mood from the beginning, it does not get any better from this situation, and it did not. It became a day when I and another bad boy ran into the pile on each other, properly. As a result, they decided to put myself in isolation.

The isolation, yes, nobody wants to sit there. In my case, I was picked up by VB Lina and locked on the isolation. Then came the Criminal Investigator on a daily basis and then they decided to move me to another prison, and then I thought okay, that's not so dangerous. But now it did not go 1 day, and not 2, not 10, no 17 days went on isolation. No, human is not. If you are sitting on the isolation for a long time, you get a little boiled in your head. You have no one to talk to, except you self. You can not do that much, you can certainly watch TV. But you can not do much more. At the moment we had no loop, we could not watch movies but just watch TV, and in the days there are not so many TV shows that are good, because we did not have a bigger selection. No, surely many say, you should not have because you are criminals, but you insist on isolation, so you sit there. Now there are surely many who say that you blame yourself, yes, you may do that. But you who say so, I think I'll think of again. To sit on the isolation is a rather tough decision.

Anyway, it went 10, 12 days, and every day the other was the same. It was a guard once a day and asked if I wanted to go out and then I had to go out in the afternoon because I could not meet anyone else. Then I had just like any other legal right to have an hour's walk a day. It started to get cold outside, well, it was not that great. I went out a few 20-30 minutes ago, you entered again. There was not much to hang in the Christmas tree. I did not think it was fun, you had lost life expectancy. If you insist on isolation, it does not matter and what the hell is going to happen, should I write a letter or. You can not write to anyone. Everything is guarded so no, for my part, it was most to lie and rest and calm down. But it became quite boring after 17 days, I can say that. After 12 days, the securityguard Mattias came up, a pretty good guard, although he was a guard, he was quite good as a person. A healthy and intelligent person. Then came VB Lina with lots of paper that I would write on, she is very nice. But it's a lady who can, as she said, she can fry like a butter in a hot frying pan, if she really wants to. Both VB Lina and the securityguard Mattias wondered how it had happened, and Mattias asked me if I had liabilities to that person. Is he completely drunk or? I do not have any debts. But that was his way of solving the situation, asking a question he would do. But in this case he was totally wrong. In both cases, Lina and Mattias, they wanted me to move to another prison as soon as possible. Now it was Criminal Investigators decision to get me moved as quickly as possible, and probably she did not think it was so acute, and then she chose to write to the Placement Unit where she apparently did not speed up the case. Although she accelerated the case, she did not write that it was acute. Then after 12 days, the securityguard Mattias came and asked if I could move back on hospital again. Well, why did I ask? They meant that I would soon be in another place, and then it would be better to live there because there were others who would isolate, and that was a strange feeling. I would move to another prison and above all, I would come from the isolation to the infirmary where I would sit, but it would be a few days there too. For this case, it was obviously not a priority. Yes, as you understand again, I had to install myself and now I was pretty tired of it. Simon who sat there when I got there at the prison for the first time. I got his old cell, and it was a pretty special feeling. It was much more humane to sit on the hospital than on the isolation. you could be 2, there was a coffee maker, everything. The question was just how long I would sit there, would I sit there for 1 day or 3 days. No, I got to sit there for 5 days. 5 days are long if you wait for something to happen. The day before we left, VB Lina came and asked me to pack my stuff in the blue box as it was called. It was about 20-25 kilograms that you had to put in the box. VB Lina walked into her office, and we packed my stuff and she weighed them. There were two boxes. Then I had to go back to my cell and VB Lina locked me in again. There were a lot of lockouts during this time. But I had actually used to myself, I did not care so much about locking. The question was only, I wanted to know what prison I would come to, but they did not know that and VB Lina knew nothing. VB Andre did not know anything either. So you had to live in uncertainty. I think it was 3 days before moving, I did not know at that time, but about 3 days before I had applied for super vised permission, and then there would be 2 guards. This was the last guarded permit so I actually had to wear a female guard in civilian clothes, and it was a very special feeling of getting into society. Here you sit at a café with a guard. I know that when we left the prison, it felt very strange. You would wear the seat belt yourself, otherwise it would be the guards who did it, but now it was me who had to do it. We were going out through the gates, then we came to the city. I sat there and wondered, oh well, what should you do now? It is called that you get an aeration. An aeration may be that you go to the doctor or the like with a few guards, but now this was a permission. We would have to walk around town for 6 hours and it may sound bad for a long time, but I can say that now it went fast. I know the guard Milla who went with me asked where I wanted to go, and I said I wanted to go to a cafe. I came to a cafe where we sat down, and there was such a buzz on every fronter so there was no way to hear anything. You was used to the fact that it was completely silent in the cell and suddenly it was so buzzing, I heard absolutely nothing and then I became brainwashed quite quickly. I was so tired of all the new impressions that I could now agree. I told Milla that I wanted to leave. She understood that I had difficulty focusing because it was Such a buzz inside. We went out after we drank the coffee. We went out to town and it was much calmer there. We walked around a bit, I looked a little in the window, the guard Milla asked how it feels. Yes, it was honestly quite mixed feelings, I did not know what to believe or think. It felt good to be out in freedom, at the same time it felt wrong, felt very shame that you would be part of this society. The day you can work. There was a long time left but as I said, I had my permission ladder and this was the last step.

Anyway, we went around, looking at different things. We did not do much. We could have gone to the movies or something but one thing I wanted was where I wanted to go back to the prison and relax. It may sound strange, but it actually was. You will actually be injured institutionally when you have been in an institution for a long time. The permission began to come to an end and Milla asked if we were going back to the prison, and I thought that was a good suggestion. I can not understand it today that I thought it was a good suggestion, but I actually thought so. We started to go to the car as Milla had been parked in a parking garage. We had not parked in the parking garage, which Milla walked towards, and I did not feel like the city so we walked around like Stevie Wonder both of us and were looking for a car that the correctional had. Now it was just because we did not find the car because we were in the wrong place. We had to ask people were a certain street low, then we went there and then we found the carpark and the car. Incredible. Anyway, we jumped into the car and started go to the prison. The closer we arrived, I felt how the pulse went down. It's strange, but it is, and so it was. I felt like home, I would come home to an prison, completely incomprehensible. Anyway, we stood there in front of the gate outside the prison and the CV (Central Guard) had to open the gate. He did it and we drove in and then it was the usual routines, and it felt safe. Then you knew what was going on. It was changing clothes, writing on paper, going through all the routines that were available. I was treated by VB Andre, then Mattias there was as safe as a living heartburn. No, sorry Mattias. Anyway late, we passed VB Linas office, she asked clearly if the permission had gone well, because we had not be able to run after you, she said. No, you did not need it. I came back volunteered, it feels good. I went in to change, and went back to my cell, and when I came in there and they locked I thought it was very nice. How to feel like it, but I thought so, and I was very tiered after all the impressions that had been in town. Soon it was locked up and the guards got into the hospital a little later than 19:45 because they locked in the department first then the hospital. I can say that the routines were quite monotonous even in the hospital. Although I thought it felt good and safe to be there, it was. VB Lina came and told me a day later that I would move to another prison.

Now it turned out that they would move me 75 miles from this prison I was sitting on, and then you might wonder, you might call it a knock (move). They say it was not a move but I've been bothered hard to believe it.

Anyway the day came when I was moving. There were quite mixed feelings both for me and for the guards because I was an inventor of this prison. I was the one who had been sitting the longest here now. Sometimes it became a bit heavy, new routines would have been established and that was something new that I faced. I was picked up by VB Lina, transport was there and they would put a handcuff on me. Then VB Lina said that I did not need any handcuffs. To sit at 75 miles with handcuffs had been quite boring. Anyway, we carried my boxes out. I took goodbye of the CV, the VB and the guards. It was a little strange, but so it was. I jumped into the car and left off the prison. Then it was 75 miles away. It's a bit special when transporting for transport is like this, they must not even stop the car more than on a custody or at a police station. Otherwise, do not let them stay.

Chapter 44: Fluid-Driving Medicine

It's a bit difficult when you're on a fluid-drive when you're going to sit 30-40 miles straight up and down without getting to the bathroom. So I told them you have to stop the bus. No, we can not stop the bus. But the fact is that they did it in a forest and I had to go out and hit a seven (pee), and that was damn nice. Then there was no more stop. There was a stop in the custody where I was going to sleep over the night and went in and lay me in the bed. It felt quite monotonously boring, sad, gray. I do not know why it felt so. Anyway, it was a toilet on the detention, and that was fine. I was there and, yes, how it felt, we should say sad. But still I was on my way to another prison. I went and settled in the night, then I went to bed, and I was really tired. In the morning, the door opened and a guard said good morning, as usual. Then we had breakfast, coffee and the like, medicine. Because we would have to go with transport again. We went away from the custody and I think we stayed in Gävle, small town in Sweden. Because the guards had to have their lunch, we had to stay there. Then we entered a small cell, difficult to describe, but there were two walls and a door and a sloping ceilings, a wooden bench and a small table stuck in the wall where you could have lunch. There would be about 1 hour. Lastly, they would come a transport and pick us up again for us to leave. Now it was just that I had to sit there for about 3 hours because there had been an accident on one of the roads. Those who drove the car could not get over because of this. The guard on the custody came to my lunch room and explained to me that they were delayed and he never thought it took more than 1 hour and now it took 3 hours. They were on your way, but I still had to sit there waiting, and it was not so great fun. To sit in such a room is not so funny, there is absolutely nothing to do, there is only a wooden bench. But finally they came, everyone was supposed to have shackles but I did not need it because VB Lina had said that it was not necessary, thankfully. So I had to go, and the others were stuck. After a few hours we were on custody I was going to sleep and at last I got a well-deserved sleep. In the morning we had breakfast and then the transport guys wanted to go to the prison I will sit on. I went to bed to sleep. I was quite tired after entering the toilet. Just doing my steering took quite a bit of my power. I lay down on my bed and felt how comfortable I wanted to sleep. Next time I opening my eyes it was morning. The time was almost 5:30 in the morning. It was just over an hour before the guards would unlock my cell. I was quite tired and did not want to go up even though I knew I had to get to the toilet. That I could only be so tired is because you are afflicted with brain fatigue. Something I have to realize I'm suffering from.

Just a thought!

I clearly thought that a person on the correctional was just an authority that handled interns, in order to get money from the government. The correctional service has no evidence of internal control. They act as authority to ensure that a person deserves a punishment, but then the rest is crazy. My own trust in the correctional is so bad that there is not even a scale. Some people should leave their services immediately, as they are directly unsuitable. Persons who display such disrespect may not have high service. When such people get high-quality services, they color the entire existing environment, and we have a very bad society. Society as You, who reads these lines, lives in. That only the government can see between the fingers when an authority spends money and violates the law. Do not think you need to say more. That the government does not see that the correctional violates the law, or they choose not to see. At the time of writing, there are about 3000 bad boys sitting on the prison a year. Perhaps the correctional wants to keep the statistics in order to get money from the government. It's not that I dont have many thoughts and theories. I have spent two years on the prison, and yet it's way to muck. After muck, there will be one year of surveillance, so you'll be in the prison for a while. Although my old criminal heart thinks that the correctional has done a lot of bad things to me personally, there are a lot of good people in the correctional.

Back to my life story ... A very good person in the correctional that I had a lot to do with is Milla, the production handler. Milla is for you who reads these lines, as a living energy force, which is running most of the time. To describe Milla, makes it easier for you to read these lines, seeing her like a thunderbolt that travels in a room and as a person is difficult to stop. In order for you to read and understand what I mean, I have some examples. Every day, Milla will come and pick me up at 9:00 and 14:00, when I work in the laundry so I can meet the other bad boys. For the most part it works. However, I thought I would tell you a few times, as it did not work.

1st example The time will be 9:00 and Milla will pick me

up on the laundry. The time will be fifteen minutes over 9:00 and in through the door comes a storm. A storm that just cleaned a silo on sawdust and the whole Milla was full of sawdust. Northlady as she was, she did not say many words. Only words like: Have cleared a silos on sawdust, there was a lot of chips frozen, so I had to use the crowbar. Can you read this, paint a painting, and in front of you, you see a woman with a crowbar at the top of a silo, pretending to forget to pick me up. Maybe she had the following thoughts. Oh, you should have a scooter so you can ... In her language. Now I've forgotten Jesper!

But I will return to Milla. Back to the correctional!

Just one thought I had ... Only before I tell you more, I want you to read, knowing that only my own values are included. So what others think is not included in this book.

Back to my life story.

The correctional has a regulatory framework that they do not follow. They have a system that the correctional uses and which is terribly square. Even the guards do not think so much happens. So it's the bad boys who get the bang, and that means that all the guards must follow a rule that really does not work at all. It will be when the correctional has a top management / system. The question is, where is the fingertip sensation that the routine guards worked after many years. A top-down system does not provide space for the guards for many years, and their experience unfortunately is not something they can use. It's not the guys and the women in the backpack corridor that make the big change, it makes the guard with fingertip feeling. Is convinced that you do not need to be a rocket scientist to figure this out.

Production Handler Milla.

Has today worked with the production handler Milla. It is a real challenge to do that. As I said earlier, I perceive her as a real irrigation that has many iron in the fire. But that's Milla. It was a lot of shelves that were supposed to be up, and some were a little crooked, so it was very difficult for two sections to fit together. Some violence was required and tools were required. The problem resolved with Milla's help was very bad. A corner pole to a shelf that would be in place. Do you think that these lines read that this would stop Milla's production manager? No way ... Although this corner post was too long or kind of too long, just Milla picked up a big hammer and with some violence ... and so little fuss, then this problem was solved. We will return to Milla.

I thought talking about a guard that made a big impression on me. Ann-Kristina, or even called "Miss ECG". To you wondering why she is called "Miss ECG" is because her mood goes upside down. So, "Miss ECG" felt the right one. At the time of writing, I have honestly not much time with her, even though she impressed me personally. It is guaranteed her mood, which apparently governs how she will be like a person! You can clearly see what mood she is on. One does not even have to wonder because she is so clear about it. If Ann Kristina is stressed, one can see it on her facial expression that becomes very ignorant. Fortunately, all doors are locked on this closed facility. Had Ann Kristina been able to, she had undoubtedly gone through these doors when she was stressed. I personally experience Ann-Kristina as very good.

Had been on my own permission eight hours for dinner and drinking coffee, when Milla appeared in my mind. How can you only get a thought of what happens on the prison when you are in permission? Incredible! Honestly, so the first thing that appears is what this production handler is doing now?

Is there any person who can find a lots of hell, it's Milla, production handler, when she's wild like a breeze. When I stood at the gate the taxi arrived at the prison, I told the guy who drove the taxi that he was calling at the gate so that the resume could open the gate. He went off the taxi. I was still in the taxi, and then I got a new thought on this production handler Milla. Once again, did I wonder what she had done when I was in permission?

But we will return to Milla...

Have now talked to Ann-Kristina or "Miss ECG" in the morning, as she is also called. After our conversation, I understand why. She is as she is, and I can also understand that as a reader you would like to know the reason why a woman does. The reason I know, and it will follow me until I get a "Earth with geothermal heat". Do not think it's relevant and add anything in my book, if I'd tell you. Then it is totally disrespectful to a person to hang out this person since this person is kind and friendly. Man shall as one shows respect and respect for a woman. To see Ann-Kristina be happy, probably made most bad boys in a better mood, and to see "Ms. ECG" pulling on the smileys and see how her nostrils rise to the sky, makes you believe Ann-Kristina has been drinking Red Bull. She will be a sweet and beautiful puma ... though she's a guard. Being able to sit alone in a taxi, thinking of a production handler who works on the prison, once permission has been granted, why do you do that when you were in person as a person? Had Milla made such a big impression on me? Or was it because we stood the gate to the prison ... Yes, it certainly wondered the researchers as well. all as one shows respect and respect for a woman.

One thing is for sure, and its that Milla has the heart in the right place. Milla knows what it's like to have a stroke, so I do not need to explain to her. She knows when I'm getting tired, and helps me with the laundry in the silent. Milla is smart, and have a lot of fingertips. Although Milla has many iron in the fire and is usually stressed, she sees what is needed and is human. As you understand, I work in the laundry for the days so it rolls on. Today, Client Handler Törnkvist was with paper I would write when I applied for open office. Client Handler Törnkvist wanted me to read these papers. The correctional described a heavily criminal person who was about me. The first thing I thought was that it was a madman and a real pig ... Had to tell Törnkvist, the Client Handler, that it was actually before I had a stroke, and that had changed for the better.

Chapter 45: Open institution

Client Handler Törnkvist's answer, where he thought I had changed my mind. I've got it, if you think it's self. The question is whether society thinks so, or if they still see a criminal who wants their work. For just so is society. Said and done. The papers are signed and the request for relocation to open institution is a fact. Now it's just time to wait, the placement unit has two weeks to go, then it will be transported to open institution. Meanwhile, I'm waiting for work in the laundry, with Stefan (Finnock) who will take over for me we are moving to new houses so there is a lot to do. There were a lot of pants and sweaters to be moved. Fortunately, Milla, the production handler helps. I'm sure it took a lot longer time if Milla did not help. All pants, sweaters and boxershorts must be folded again ... Then we're not talking about 150 pieces just. Now there are several hundreds, which will once again be folded. I seemed fold together and there were hundreds left. Another intake, (Finnock), helped me, because my balance is poor after the stroke I had. He got up on the ladder standing there and took off all the plastic on the new things I was having trouble with. He really helped me with everything I had trouble doing. Guards, VB and the Criminal Investigator found it to be good. Production Handler Milla and I, like intaken, had proven to doing a good job, which everyone in the staff thought looked good. The guard Adde who was responsible for the laundry looked completely satisfied. He probably was both surprised and shocked at the same time, as there was nothing to get in the laundry. We went together, into the new store where everything was now. The guard Henke thought it had been settled and done now. He thought it was bad before, so now he was satisfied.

Chapter 46: The Priest Anna

Today, Pastor Anna came here and invited cakes. It's a priest, I think have a healthy attitude to life. She would work in the correctional, as this priest sees reality, and not the square rules that the correctional System consists of. The priest Anna is human who probably sees what would be needed in the correctional. Anna has the ability to see and hear the individual who needs to come to life. I have not met so many people in the correctional that have that ability. The priest Anna also have a big fingertip feeling. I am delighted with my old crime heart. Pretty sad to meet the priest Anna on the prison. Had it been better if I meet this person in freedom ... but so is life.

Today, there was a lot to do in the laundry, so Finnock and I worked on, so we should catch up. We were sort the laundry, like those boxer shorts that were so boring with dirt ... showed up! Finnock was simply not impressed by these boxer shorts. I found that these boxer shorts content was really bad. What Finnock also did. Finnock now understands why wearing gloves is important. The weekend that was 21st and 22nd was very bad for me as a person.

Woke up in the morning and had a lot of pain in the heart, which meant I went to my contactman, guard Krille. Above this I had toothache. My contactman Krille went straight to VB Torsten. VB Torsten made a direct decision, send me to prisondoctor, and they had to make the tests that needed to make a decision to go to the hospital.

The ambulance arrived, and they connected a lot of machines. How to oxygenate and then I was shaved on my chest so they could take an ECG. Sitting and reading these lines makes it difficult for me to influence you. But the following happened.

Chapter 47: Heart & ECG

My ECG looked good said the ambulance driver, however, my blood pressure was too high and pain in my chest, making them want me to go to the hospital. There was a ride in an ambulance and soon we were in the hospital. Throughout the journey, the new ambulance wrote done all the medications I took. He also saw how I oxygenated me and my blood pressure. They saw that my blood pressure was too high and had sent my ECG to the hospital. Once in the hospital, I had to lay on another bed.

The nurse that received was nice to me, and rolled me into a department and would begin a lot of sampling by taking blood samples. Now it was just a small problem ... Knitting me was very difficult. The first nurse knit me in my arm and hand, and then she asked if someone had stuck me in the feet. No, no one had done that. You clearly saw how my guard Krille pulled himself up and his forehead looked like a raisins. The guard Krille sat on a chair side of my bed. It was the first time, I saw how the chair he was moving on, the more he pulled up. The nurse says there will be a little bit knit of my foot. You can now see how my contact person Krille lifts a foot, as he understands it hurts very much.
Can you read ... see a contact person lifting a foot and pulling himself up so that he could be fostered because of pain. The nurse is not satisfied with the fact that there is not much blood, which then turns on the needle that is in my foot, and it did really hurt. For those who read, understand the pain, it's like bending the elbow in the wrong

direction. Now the pain was boring high, but I did not say a word. Had the nurse asked if it hurt, I´d said the pain is very low, and it hardly feels.

The truth is, it really hurts! The nurse asks another nurse to take the samples, so she walks out of the study room we were in. Meanwhile, as the second nurse came to the study room we were in, my contactman Krille told me to avoid knit people in the feet when the pain was very high. If you had to knit people in their feet, you should use as little needle as possible. According to my guard Krille, the needle I was exposed to was very rough. He thought it was a "Horse needle" and it was not a good day for me in coming, the new nurse and will be taking blood samples. She had talked with the other nurse that gave up. So this nurse saw this as a good test to try their skills, and she tells me a lot of times before she gets blood. She said there was a good blood vessel in my left arm, on the inside. She looks very happy, and I also did not have to go through this hell again. Taking these samples was necessary, so the doctor could see if my heart was injured and leaked. It would take about 1.5 hours before we knew what the samples showed. VB Torsten had probably called twice on guard Krille's phone, when Krille silently phoned his phone, who understandably did not hear these calls. VB Torsten would like to know if I were to stay in the hospital, which should mean that VB Torsten had to call in staff who could sit in the hospital at night. When the samples came, the doctor told me that my samples looked good. The doctor thought I had an infection in the muscle around the heart. Had it been the heart you can not affect pain by pressure. I had to go home to the prison again, and that was good. Happyest was probably VB Torsten who did not have to call in staff. We went to the waiting room to be picked up by the guard Sanna!

Sanna came and picked us up and drove us to the prison. It was a walk when we got to the prison and then a VB should not say that the gate should open. VB Torsten then goes out to secure the place and says that they can open the gate, even if it was a walk. VB Torsten is one who would like to point with his entire arm. In this matter, VB Torsten left himself and secured the area and then took a decision to open the gate. VB Torsten is a real paragraph rider but this old man has a fingertip feeling and I think it's good. If VB Torsten is looking happy, it must be in prison teams, otherwise VB Torsten will not. VB Torsten opened the door so I could go back to the prison again. I was glad to be on the prison again and VB Torsten looked happy too. Everyone was happy because everything gone well. Even my guard Krille looked happy.

VB Torsten would know that there was liquor gel on the toilet. Then Torsten would be blocked by the whole hospital, taking all the liquor jelly. So he had not developed a stomach ulcer. Then he would have called in people.

Yesterday, The guard Greg came with permission papers, when I went to the dentist. The guard Greg went and picked up the car we were going to go in. Meanwhile I was waiting, the new guard Livia came and would make sure I wrote the decisions and permission papers that were needed. The guard Greg came and we went out to the car.

The guard Greg opened the car door so I could jump into the car. The guard Livia walked around the car and even jumped in the car. Livia did not say much about the trip to the dentist. Probably because she is Norwegian. Or she's just shy ... We were soon at the dentist, which lay about ten minutes from the prison. Well in place, we went in, and behind me Greg went, and onward went Livia. When we entered a bit, the guards Livia and Greg were unsure where we were going. I stand in the middle of Greg and Livia. Livia wanted to go one way and Greg in the other direction. Livia asked a dentist nurse and as usual, a woman had a right again ... Typically!

We were going to that way what Livia wanted. We went to the lift and went to level three, where the dentist lay. The guard Greg went off the elevator first, then me and later, the guard Livia. When we entered the waiting room we would sit and wait for, I would write my social security number and Livia was kind enough to do it when I was having trouble with the stroke I had. Now you are inscribed, Livia said, so we went and sat down. Greg and I sat directly. Greg is an ice bear and likes being cool. He thought it was very hot in the waiting room we were in. Livia went to see if there was a newspaper. She came back with a World of Science. She liked best about the World History of Science. It was not much said when I was called to the dentist. So we started going! First there is Livia, me in the middle and Greg, the great polar bear went behind. Once inside the dentist, I greeted her. Her name was Hanna and looked very kind. Livia and Greg waited outside, meanwhile. The dentist Hanna, noticed that I was stiff as a securitybox when she examined me. Dental doctor Hanna wanted to take some pictures so she wanted pictures on the root and the tooth ... Dentist Hanna understood that it was not so nice to bite together. After a while, Hanna got a picture, but if she was satisfied? I do not think so! After looking at the pictures, dentist Hanna said those magical words I did not want to hear. You should root canal your teeth ... said dentist Hanna! No! I answered directly, and felt a certain concern for this mess. Do not think it hurts to make a root canal. It's more about thinking about the pain you had before, said dentist Hanna. Just to hear how a root canal is going to make time stand still and I became as stiff as a Franz Jäger security-box. When she explained, came the guard Greg and the guard Livia. They looked happy and nice. I looked more pale. The pain had dentist Hanna removed, so she was really worth a good day, and her colleague. I went back to the prison with Greg and Livia, so it became more a regular day on the prison. Everything went well, though I was at the dentist.

Chapter 48: The guard Niclas

Today in the morning, I went down with the guard Niclas. He is always nice, and it sounds natural to talk a little with him. The guard Niclas and my big son are very similar. To see Niclas almost every day made me think of my great son Tobias. Had not Niclas had a beard, then one might have thought that my great son, Tobias had been a guard. Tobias wants to be Police and is looking for a police school ... myself, I am an international bad boy, and who is the only one who is criminal in the family.

Just a thought!

Should film my grandchild with the mobile phone that was on the couch and he leaned against the window. I started filming, and told my grandchild to say something. Then he began to cautiously sound a word that began with the letter P. I apologized for saying Daddy that all children do. Then my grandson says Police when I'm film. I had to ask what he said and then my grandchild said it again ... Police ... It was an experience to hear this word from my grandchild.

Return to the guard Niclas!

I experience the guard Niclas as a cautious person, who does not take shit, he is kind but not stupid. He is probably a person who does not sounded so much. Niclas is quite silent. This is if he doesn´t know a person. It's quite hard to notice Niclas. He never claims so there are not so many vowels and consonants from him. Niclas has a good and bright side, which almost never requires his dark side to enter. Is completely convinced that Niclas is good can display a very dark page, if necessary. Although he is, a very nice person.

In the morning I talking with Client Handler Törnkvist about the move to open institution tomorrow. They would have a meeting on the placing unit now in early March, said Törnkvist. This would mean that I'm at the earliest on open office on 12th March, according to Client Handler Törnkvist.

Just a thought!

It's a weird feeling when I think of an open institution. I have not been out for a few years in society and it is not, but I feel a little worried about this. All new impressions and experiences are all new to me. So it's a life that I personally do not use.

Back to the move ...

Getting to open institution certainly requires new routines, and future goals. Coming to a new place, taking a lot of energy from me as a person. Just hope I enjoy the new facility, and with them new bad boys that's on the prison. At the same time, it's mixed feelings to leave "Laundry" now when everything is in place as I want it. Finnock is the person who will take over after me in the laundry. Finnock is orderly and polite, just as I am, so it will be fine. Sadly, it will be a mess again.

Production Handler Sari is a person I had a lot to do. I thought describe Production Handler Sari so you as reading can feel this person a bit better. I perceive Sari as a person close to the laugh. When she laughs she pulls her eyes together and blushes a little, then she laughs. She´s laugh loud and spontaneously, which concerns most people. She is both a good listener, a speaker and it's not common with a person.

Although Production Handler Sari has a lot of work on her agenda, but she takes time. Wants to believe she is spontaneous, in her entire way, and it implies that she is a person as a whole. You can look at someone if it is listening, and if the subject is interesting. Then you have a fixed look and look straight ahead. If you are not interested, you are sweeping with your eyes and, at worst, looking down at the left during a conversation, avoiding saying what you think. It's not good at all. Production Handler Sari is not a person looking to the left during our conversations, I think that is good. Sari never interrupts if you speak. There are very good qualities I think and it shows that Sari, has a healthy attitude to life and she shows the person in question the respect that it deserves. At the time of writing, I can not say anything negative about the Production Handler Sari who only shows a good page. Hopefully it never changes under my mind. Production Handler Sari deserves to be respected.

Production Handler Jan is a fun person, and is like a class clown who makes fun moves. Mr. Jan is a very serious person who can be funny for a second and demanding a second next second. Production Handler is just what Mr. Jan is. Yes, when. So maybe it's not that weird that he can turn of a penny. Probably, his work requires him to be so.

It can not be easy to sit on two chairs. Do not have anything negative to say about Mr. Jan.

One day on the laundry!

Today there were three bad boys who dropped their baskets. Finnock went straight to these baskets, and as we started washing immediately. The bad boys wants to get their baskets back in the morning when it's Friday. So Finnock really lay in, he'll take over after me. Want to record an event that happened during yesterday. The guards came with a basket full of laundry. As a starter. It belonge to a friend of mine who had a move. Which I did not know until we had dinner at 4:00 PM, then my friend did not come! What the hell had happened? What happens? Hope he can hear by letter, so I can find out why he got a move. Annoying not knowing anything. The guards say nothing like usual. So is life on the prison. That a friend gets a move is not fun and it affects me very negatively, as a person. Notice in my mood that I was like a ticking bomb that would love to get off. I asked one oft he intaken if he knew what had happened. Then he answered the following: I'm not working here! Idiot, that was the word I answered him with, and was really angry, but went straight away. My mood is my weak side, and in the evening that inyaken came when I was playing chess, so I apologized for what I told him. He realized that you could not be in a good mood all the time. That a friend gets move is boring and it was costing me a move if I did not leave the place. Thank goodness, I did.
Describing Finnock is not so easy, as he has apparently

many strings on his lyra. Finnock is a good listener who is
also a diplomat in the fingertips. He likes to listen to other
people's problems. Probably, most people trust Finnock
who really has one good heart He tries to solve their possible problems by first listening to the situation and then
looking at their problems with other eyes who hopefully
solve this. Finnock is a person who has very hard to say
no. It now attracts people who should show Finnock more
respect than to ask for services. Some people certainly see
Finnock's knowledge as an asset, and do not respect him
with his knowledge. The fact that he is a diplomat is no
doubt.

The guard Vicky helped me down today, she seems nice.
Can not say how she is like a person. A little hard when
you have had no so much time with Vicky. Describing the
guard Vicky is almost impossible, as I honestly do not
know how she is a person. I think Vicky is a person who
wants to help all the bad boys so they get a good future if
it works. What I know is that Vicky adheres to the law
and what is not in the prison law is under development ...
want to say that fingertip feeling is an insecure card for
this careful general ...

Chapter 49: The guard Henke & Dentist

I would go to the dentist and the guard Henke to practice his routine. There were three guards that went. Which means that this trip to the dentist requires increased security. I have entered permissions, so this security was only for the guard Henke would get his routine. The guard Henke picked up the bus we were going to go with. In the bus, I jump, Adde and finally Greg. The guard Henke, who was a truck driver, ran well and safely. When we came at the dentist, Greg starts off first, then Adde and I last. It was that the guard Greg started to go first, and then the guard Adde, then I and last the guard Henke.
Inside the waiting room I would sit in, there were two people. In comes three guards and me. These two people who were already sitting there only looked up once, then they did not do the more. Was summoned by the dentist, so the guard Greg went with me. They thought I had some kind of infection. The dentist pressed on nearby teeth, and the pain was very high. She was pretty sure I had an infection after the look of the pictures she took. The dentist wrote out mouth rinse that I would take twice a day for ten days.
When I got ready by the dentist, we went to the prison again. I went out from the dentist, and there was the guard Adde and the guard Henke. We went to the bus all four, and as I got there to the dentist, the guards helped with the support of the stairs. We had yet another short trip. We were back on the prison again. Everything had gone well.

Would like to describe the difference between Henke and Adde. That there is a big difference between these guards is a fact. I want to start by describing the guard Henke, who I think is a natural and human person. Henke can if he wants to be a true article rider. However, I do not feel that it is in his nature. I think he is a good and fun person and it feels good to talk to him. I have nothing negative to say about the guard Henke ... maybe it might be that he gets better in Skåne or buy a dictionary.

Adde is like VB Torsten, who would like to point with his entire hand. Adde has good pages too ... just do not know what! Nah! The guard Adde, now I'm kidding well. It is certainly not wrong with rules, and as intake the life of the prison becomes a little harder. It's probably good and bad. Adde is responsible for purchasing the laundry, so a regulatory framework is required. At the time of writing, I have nothing negative to say about Adde.

Worked in the laundry ...

Another day on the laundry and I do it on the routine, though I'm sitting on the prison. Every day I go to the laundry, want to say to my job, become a routine. For my volta (punishment), it becomes shorter for each day and I am pleased with my old carnal heart. When the bad boys leaves their laundry baskets, there's a piece of numbers, with their cell number, so I know who's wearing these sweaters and pants. Some of the bad boys have private boxershorts and socks, so it had become messy otherwise. To wait and see that these machines will be ready make sure you have time to write. Big parts of this book are written on the prison. So right now I write these lines on the prison, in the laundry .... At the time of writing, Finnock seeks a dictionary as time passes. He is a good old man who has a good heart, making him very nice. Probably it will be a placement decision during the day tomorrow. Are some mixed feelings for open institution. Probably, Client Handler Törnkvist receives a message soon, where I will be placed. As I understood on Client Handler Törnkvist, I can move as soon as I finish a module. But that's the placing unit, deciding, Client Handler Törnkvist, did not I would worry.

Talked to my contactman Lelle about the move to open institution. My contact person called the Client Handler Törnkvist directly and he told my contact person that Törnkvist had spoken to them on the placing unit that I had a seat on an open institution on the 12th of March after completing the module within the crime break and those on the placing unit made a preliminary decision as you know. The decision itself comes to the 12th of March. So, my contact, Lelle, thought I would go on to the crime break.

Today, the placement unit has a meeting about where to sit. Having special conditions is quite decent. It's fine in some cases, so you get an individual review, that might be good for me I think.

Chapter 50: Work with Finnock

Today, Finnock and I finished the laundry, so we made a commonly decision to enter the mechaniworkshop. It was not or no work to perform so most of the bad boys that were there did not even go to the workshop. Finnock and I went back to the laundry again. It was a heavy day. I was awaiting a message from the placing unit about where to sit. This afternoon, crime break will it be for my part. Just hope that the day rolls in the normal order. Then I'll meet Jeppe, also called Jesper. To go on crime break claims up a lot of emotions and it takes a lot of energy of me as a person. Probably, the correctional wants to have this reaction by us. You have their hopes that, as a person, I will get a better mood and maybe my fuse will be further through these courses ... who knows!

Today at the crime break, we received two papers we would write down on how we solved difficult situations. Different scores from 0-4 and also write the technique we used. We are currently writing two bad boys and we have two program leaders who are very good. Notice that they have great routine to those oldtimers. It's probably the first thing I'm watching if the program leaders read only in a book to complete this course. It's like all people who can play notes and make it sound good. A really good musician can play on the ear and feeling. Just like these program leaders, they can do the most of their feelings, but also gather the facts in a book. They are really good.

Have today been helped down the stairs of the guard Jan who is also a production leader. Talked to the guard Jan well before it was down, that there was no breakfast in the fridge. The guard Jan would raise the question at the meeting, now in the morning. So we'll see how it goes. So yet another day on the laundry, was a fact. Today, my regular contactman came down because he started working after 11:00. Think we were just as happy because Lelle had been training for two weeks. We talked the most of about my location on open institution. Then my contactman needed to go because he had a lot to do. He was talking to Criminal Investigator when the Client Handler was available this day. Lelle is very good and I really trust him. He tries to resolve problems immediately. Lelle is a real oldtimer, which actually begins to come up in the years. The fact that Lelle contactman starts coming up over the years actually has big advantages. One can then replace the battery in his hearing aid and replace his glasses as he usually wears his nose. :) Then neither does or does the old man see or hear that much, and then he is taken as a resident of a license application. Contactman Lelle and I have had some time together and trust has begun to grow. Right now, when confidence is good, I'm going to open institution, strange life is. My time on the prison is starting to end and my trip has now made a mark in the Criminal Care. Me and my contact person Lelle have really gone through the most things you can do. Some days I thought it was the most crazy, then my friend Lelle was there, who saw the possible problem with quite different eyes, and we resonated about problems encountered and usually resolved. My contactman was never stressed by any problem. Was he stressed at some point, old Lelle, that was if there were no dictionary words and that did not happen so often. I had some letters on data

and my contact person Lelle always read what I had written and replaced all the Scandinavian words that I wrote.
It was very kind of Lelle to do it.

Just a thought!

Yesterday when I was going to get up from the laundry,
Milla and Sari production handler helped me up. They
thought I had made progress and I could now both go and
talk, and it was completely new to me. It's not as easy as
you think. I'm a man, so doing two things at the same
time is hard.

That the production handler who are girls can surely agree
with this. The fact is that you do not see their own progress and that can be both good and evil. Noticed myself
that I stopped in the stairs when Milla and Sari, the production handler, said that I had made progress. What a
strange man is like a person? Production handler Milla
and Sari had to pull me in my arm so I would go again.

Today, Milla production handler made a cake. It was a
great cake that could be at least five people. Now we were
only two people in the laundry, it did not prevent us from
eating the whole cake. I sought permission from my
contact person Lelle. My contact person would clearly
know where I was going to travel on my permission. Had
intended to go down to my boys in Skåne. Lelle tried to
find a flight to Malmö, which proved difficult. Just hope
he succeeds in doing it. I thought there's a lot to work now
when you want permission. Personally, there are many
thoughts I have, and I think there will be a lot of new
things to think of as a person. Today, I can call my big
son Tobias and tell me how it will be. Hope it's possible
to solve, because I've seen this to meet the guys. We'll get
to see what my contact person Lelle is coming up with,

he'll check out the travel times today. Should leave my doses to fill these with medication. Meet by my contact person Lelle and the guard Niclas. Contactman Lelle hoped that the SSK was on the prison today. The question was if I would fill in the paper to go to the dentist if the pain came back again, now that my medicine had ended. That the pain was coming back was a fact. As sure as I have to make a root canal now ...Fuck!

It is now proven that as a person you can join a root canal only the pain disappears. The guard Niclas said I would fill these papers so I could go to the dentist. The guard Niclas also witnessed my signature. According to dentist, Hanna practitioner, root canal was the option that was applicable. We will see what happens. The guard Niclas left an invoice I submitted when I would pay the invoice that was completely wrong, when I got free dentistry. The invoice is now shredded and a new invoice has been sent to the correctional.

Contactman Lelle will come down to the laundry when he knows how the flight is going. I see contactman Lelle get into the workshop, he walked to me with fast steps, I sat in the cabin and played chess with another intake. Lelle picked up a paper at times when the flight went on. I stop play chess with the intaken, so I could look at the times Lelle wrote on the paper. Under my special terms, I can apply for my 24 or 32 hours. now the 14th. Lelle had talked with Client Handler Törnkvist who thought it would be easier if I was looking for my 24 or 32 hours. On the open facility I would sit on, because I'll be there on the 12th and I have applied for permission on the 14th.

Probably, Client Handler Törnkvist has the right to ask if I will be moved before the weekend. So there was no permission for my part and will call my children and tell them. At the time of writing, I have not been home with them in two years. Contactman Lelle wanted us to complete my permission so that it was ready in my KLASS. I myself could call my big son Tobias, and tell he that the permission was canceled. It was heard that he was disappointed, and it does not feel good at all as dad to tell such a negative decision. Just hope I get permission the weekend after, so the guys can not suffer again. My contactman Lelle realized that I wanted to leave a time and date when it became. He also said that I had gone away so far and that I had to get out with a week to. I stand out, but do the children do it? Something I really think about.

Client Handler Törnkvist came down to the laundry, telling me that I had a decision to sit on open institution from 16/3 and that a guard will tell me the placement decision. Client Handler Törnkvist received the investment decision on March 3, 2015. Had to ask Client Handler Törnkvist if the program manager received the info that he should have received. It considered Client Handler Törnkvist.

Just a thought!

Sitting on a closed institution is not fun, though, it's a security. Later on an open institution gives greater freedom which is under great responsibility. It is clear that you want to sit on an open institution after year on a closed institution. After all years, I'm a little bit more careful about me. Because I am very hard to trust people, I feel very difficult to open me, as I always disturb people. So to sit on an open institution, I require people in my presence. Have today talked to my contact person Lelle, where I would be on my permission as my contact person entered the data so that they were ready when I came to open institution. My contact person Lelle would check with Client Handler Törnkvist if I could go to open institution before the date of service. My contact person Lelle would check what was applicable and then come down to the laundry. At the time of writing, I do not know how it will be.

My contact person Lelle and I had a very good conversation about what I would do in the future. Contactman Lelle thought I would join the writers' union, although some were nerds, I could build new networks. My contactman, Lelle, is a god man who is actually entitled to open a number of doors by joining the writers' union and maybe part of my new network.

Have now talked with my Contactman Lelle, who had talked with Client Handler Törnkvist who told me that I could not move before the date of the placement decision, so it will be a weekend at the closed institution.

Chapter 51: Crime-breaking

Has today been on the crime-break and talked about different solutions, and how to solve these problems. Mr. P as going to hold some role play, and at the time of writing, I will not say it's a comfortable thought. We will expose ourselves to a lot of uncomfortable situations that we will manage in society that I personally do not feel I belong to. According to Mr. M, should Mr. P keep in role play and he does not want any blue eyes. Mr. P thought we had finished the module we were dealing with. Mr. P turn to Mr. M and wondered both by and verbally what Mr. M thought. Mr. M also thought we were doing this module. Jeppe and I wondered if we could see Thursday's lesson, even though we did not have to go to this lesson. Both Mr. M and Mr. P thought we could see it so.

Talked to the other Jeppe if I could order a sandwich cake for the weekend, then I will move to the Sörby institution. Had not thought about this when another intake took up the subject. Jeppe working in the kitchen would hear the chefs if it could be solved.

Had a conversation with Production Handler Sari about sitting on open institution. Sari was convinced that it would be better for me to sit there. I even had a dream about the Sörby institution and all the cows that were there. Production Handler Sari laughed and pulled his eyes together. Then she blushed and then you knows that her laughter is genuine. We had to cancel our call when a person came from the Employment Service through the door. Probably, Production Handler Sari notices that I think it's an insecure card to be on an open institution. All safety is gone. These are absolutely mixed feelings.

Today it's Thursday and it will not be crime-break because we're done with the module we'd go through. Now it
will not be. You can work in the laundry all day. It does
not matter at all, I like to work in the laundry, then I will
move to the Sörby institution.
I also had a long conversation with the priest Anna, we
talked about my future. The priest Anna thougth one
would be honest, something that may be difficult if you
do not want people in their surroundings to run from there. Any partner in the future must be honest with it. How
else would it be? As a person, one must be able to rely on
his surroundings.
What should I write in my CV? Should I be honest there?
Is quite convinced that you who read these lines understand what I mean. Should I lie in my own resume to get a
calm and safe future? No! There is no alternative for me.
Then there will be lectures about my former life. Then
there's no need to be a lot of lies.

Just a thought!

Today, I only have two days left for this institution, then
it is leaving for class 3 institution. I have always been in
closed institution and for the first time I will be sitting in
an open institution. That's a strange feeling I have. Then I
have slept badly those last days. Wake up already half
past three and can not sleep more. I think you are strange
as a person who apparently reacts. I would have liked to
sleep for a few hours, but that sleep resolved with her
absence. So it was that I looked at the ceiling and a bit on
Tv ... Terrible when I can not sleep. I was thinking about

how it would be at the new facility and how the guards were doing The things I need when you have a stroke. Hope it will be fine there.

The guard Sanna I perceive as a person who would like to address any problems right away. Sanna never takes on anything that can not be done right away. Do not know if Sanna is a bit shy. Very hard to say, when she does not show it right away. She picked me up and my Contactman Krille at the hospital. Inside the car, the guard Sanna was sitting at the steering wheel with a knitted cap over her ears and wearing small glasses. She probably frozes. To see her, make sure Sanna becomes a pretty woman and it was a bit cute to see Sanna protect herself from the cold. The guard Sanna is a good person, and it's just hoping that her working skill will get rid of more guards. Because it is true that most of them do not have a fingertip feeling and, unfortunately, some are waiting for the next paycheck. Sanna is not so at all. She is professional and fair.

Chapter 52: Milla & Sari

Have said goodbye to the girls today, or Production Handlers Milla and Sari. Sari thinks it will be a routine the more years she works at the institution. Production Handler Sari had more problems at the beginning when she started working with inmates in the institution. Sari is a Production Handler that I think is good. Production Handler Milla I have had a lot of time with. It takes a lot of time to move a lot of sweaters, boxers shorts and we did not know how it would be. It became a lot of hours and reasoning how the best result could be. In addition to the work we have done now, I hope that scheme will remain. Will miss everyone on production and some guards. Probably I will mostly miss Production Handler Milla. We have had the most time together. Milla is badly kind so she should have a higher service. Will miss some people a lot, so it's not without hurting my old carnal heart.

Today it's only a day left until I get out to open institution. It feels a bit wretched that it's actually the last night with the bad boys tomorrow. There are good guys on the leg (department) that I'm sitting on.

Mr. Jan whom I'm playing chess with is a very good old man, but it's a bit of a shame that oldtimer does not hear so good. I think I'll send new batteries to the old man. Jan and I have probably found each other and play kind of chess every day ... but would like some resistance ... Shows a little Jan. He has many good pages, Ehh! Do not

just know what! No Jan! You are a good person, and
chess player.

Jeppe and Niclas are the department's young men. Niclas,
wants sound, like a rooster, but sounds more like a seal
that sits slightly in the throat. He spits gravel all day and
thinks he carries on an invisible refrigerator. Niclas is
good and kind as a person.
Jeppe is a person who gave me a new face for ECG, for
me he is everywhere. One moment he is in the kitchen,
the next second he plays badminton, he is everywhere.
Will write more lines about him.

Chapter 53: Stoffe Chairman

Stoffe (The Bull from Bro) is a person who loves to laugh and it's loud. The best thing about him is that he laughs honestly and you see him in his eyes. Stoffe took over the chairman after me. After a few hours after being elected Chairman of the Confederation Council he came to my cell and said, "I feel cheated. I had to hear what he meant? Quote: Everyone just wants a lot, and how should I solve that would you have thought? Do you have candy, some chocolate just ...
Similarly, Stoffe is in a nutshell. He is a nice dot.

Just a thought...

 Now that I'm thinking, when the guards came in to me and submitted my blue boxes, actually the VB also came in. He wanted answers to some questions, whether I was suicidal, or the like. They have an obligation to ask such things, and I could only answer no, and then there was no more. Then it went into the department.
We jumped into the car and drove off and after a few hours on the road we were on the station long up in Norr-land. Yes, where it was, does not matter and it does not tell this story, the question is just how could they put me here. Here was a whole meter of snow. I have not seen so much snow in my entire life. I entered the institution and those from transport followed me in and handed in my blue boxes and then I received new clothes and had to

change. Then I had to come down to the department and place me in and put my stuff in. Greeted those who sat in the department, and it was a very weird prison. There were 4 - 5 people in each department. We had a small kitchenette, sofa, the most necessary one such as a small fireplace where you could cook. It was just like i had a move but I got it better, for some reason. All of a sudden we had our own stoves and the like, real cutlery, real glass, yes, the feeling was absolutely huge.

Back to my life story …

Chapter 54: The move to the open institution

Has today been moved to open institution by VB Torsten-himself. The VB who follows the prison law to the point and dot. Clearly, took the chans to ask important questions to Torsten. Old man Torsten, in fact, has a great deal of experience in the correctional service. As I understood, Torsten has been in a lot of areas within the correctional, and it gives him a broad experience. VB Torsten has been, as I understood it, in the following places. Worked on the detention for many years. He has been co-ordinator, boss, for now to be VB. In other words, Torsten has a lot of experience, so it became interesting to ask my questions to Torsten. I wanted to know how Torsten looks at the correctional Center as a whole. I also wanted to hear what values Torsten had for many years in the correctional. My first question was what the care consisted of, when it is called the Criminal Care. According to Torsten, care could be anything from VSP to the various programs that one could take. Torsten himself saw problems with the new guards (Ladybugs), had a great deal of uncertainty that did not give confidence in the bad boys. Probably, it creates only more questions and an uncertainty as an intake. VB Torsten can be as somebody, who has a boring heartburn, if he is in the mood. I had some questions I wanted to answer, and the trip was only about five miles long. In other words, I thought it was quite difficult to ask the right questions, and the time was very tight. I wanted to ask the right questions that I thought were important. Probably there are many readers who want to know what answers VB Torsten gave. I was curious about these answers myself. Since Torsten worked for many years for the detention, it was natural to ask the question of locking innocent people? VB Torsten's answer was the following

... "I have no problem with that." That he was from Norrland there was no doubt about.

Then it was quiet in the car. Suddenly Torsten breathed a deep breath, and I thought Torsten might have to answer his answer. Well! He took only a deep breath. It was quiet again in the car, and only the engine was heard. After a few hundred meters, VB Torsten began to tell you that you feel bad if you are innocently locked up on the detention. You would have done that yourself. However, I do not think it's my job to judge people. It must be the court that made the decision, said VB Torsten. On that question, I think VB Torsten is right. Because of that, you can not accuse a guard of detention, you are detained. Many people find it hard to see that these guards actually do their work, and are less appreciated. Unfortunately, there were not so many questions on the trip. When it was about five kilometers left on the journey, VB Torsten told us that the facility fed sea eagles and there were some sea eagles sitting on the fields. I have now learned that these sea eagles are about two meters between the wing tips. A really big bird. These birds can take big turns.

Back to Torsten.

I had to hear how it was on this prison. Torsten had worked on this shelf as coordinator for some time. He thought it was a good prison and a good nature. We, as we received, had many opportunities to employ us. Once upon a time, I wondered where the prison was? Given that there was nothing that told us we were on a prison. We're up,

said VB Torsten ... Incredible! I thought, here a bad boys driving in a tractor and I'm left in the car, and I'm completely paralyzed by the freedom that was on this prison and I was just used to closed institutions. I was out on an open institution and I was probably a little shocked by the freedom that was on this place. I really hope that those who read these lines will feel and understand all the new, impressions, smells and the freedom you feel when you come to open institution. The feeling you have when sitting at a closed facility is like standing out on a big meadow and having no sense of smell. To then sit on an open institution is like standing on the same flourishing meadow, with a huge sense of smell. Any impression I received when I came to this facility is about the same.
Hope you as reading understand the feeling.

After talking to VB Torsten, I left the car. Torsten was in full swing carrying a lot of boxes. In the CV (Central Guard), the guard Livia, who was with me at the dentist, was sitting. Livia and I greeted and opened the door so I could come in. Livia came to be my contact person.

Chapter 55: Open Office

I got to sit and wait in the waiting room and get some
food. There was fish today, and it was good with some
food. The guard that brought the food, I would drink some
water because I had to leave UP (urine sample) when coming to a new facility. So I had to leave the UP in a cup.
When it was left, it became enrollment. I have drawn a lot
of things over the years. The guard did not look so impressed with all the things I had. She started writing all
my things, I saw that the guard thought there were many
things. Even though she did not say that, her look was a
completely different thing. There were some things twice
and it bothered her a number of times. She had to travel a
few times and stumble around in the ment a number of
timboxes. She was focused on her task and really went for
it. I notice clearly when she was less focused. Then she
was very talkative and talked about other things. She was
an experienced person, and I do not think she takes a shit.
As I've said before, it's a very experienced guard, with a
big fingertip feeling. Unfortunately, she is unable to use
this experience in the field of the correctional. When the
enrollment was complete, we should go to the closet. I
have done this moment a number of times over the years,
so this was nothing new to me. When I was at my closet, I
locked in all my drawers in the closet. The other prison
had not sent my jacket, shoes and the sweater. These
things were in the other closet, on the other prison, therefore these things remained. The guard would call the other
prison so they could send my stuff. I had a separate eight-
hour permission and then you get a permission cabinet,

which made some of my things remain on the other prison. Such happens sometimes, and now it hit me.

The guard that made the entry went with me to my new room. I was impressed with the striking nature that this prison had. After a couple of minutes, I was at my new room that the guard showed me. It was a good room, which was not like a cell, and the view was very nice when I looking out from the window. It was quite common windows, not safety windows with bars that I used to be used to. Outside of my window there was a porch with a bench that you could sit and have your morning and evening coffee on. I used to sit there and listen to the birds and watch the deer when it was quiet. I could take long walks outside in the wild, and did not blew the wind, so it was quiet. Only my footsteps I could hear. A good fccling ...

You would only be in institution on the first week, and then you should not leave the facility. That week, it did not go right soon, but it was a rule that applied to all new people who came to the institution. I felt that you had to start landing, and there were nine other people on the same leg (department) that I had to adapt to. They were sitting here too. Partly they have been here anymore, so it became a challenge to me. I focused on arranging my new room, which I should now live in. It was quite dusty, so I started to clean, so you got what you wanted. Both on the tv and in the windowsill it was really dusty, about a millimeter of dust and that was quite a lot. Perhaps hard to understand when it should be cleaned when moving into a room. After I cleaned, I started setting up the photos on my grandchildren. Always nice to put photos on my grandchildren, although it's hard to see these photos, it's just a fact that their grandfather is sitting on the prison. I would be out with my grandchildren and buy a glass or similar to them. In any case, I should not sit on the prison, as it will be difficult to give them different things when you only have thirteen Swedish crowns per hour. Very many feelings are, of course, that I have to be able to handle. It´s not without me being affected to see the pictures of my grandchildren. Even though there are positive feelings, I get affected. I get affected by all the impressions. So concerned that I have to focus on other things. On almost my desk there are pictures of my grandchildren. There were some other things, too. In order for you as a reader to get a picture, I'll tell you what it looked like. In the middle of my desk were some photos of my grandchildren. To the right was a table lamp, on the left lay a bracelet, as it stood "Stop and Think", which was made at the Kumla institution. On the side of the bracelet on the left were stamps and a phone book, there was also my watch and there was a colaburk. Gazing with ignorance of these photos made me feel vigilant and a feeling that really hurt the depths. I'm very hard to explain how I feel that pain. How to explain how this pain is perceived is really difficult. I felt it more, like a huge pain and I was breaking into molecules. I now understand more what the artist Björn A. meant with a "Heart can go in a thousand pieces", because just so I felt it.

Want to watch and tell about a guy I was wearing during my release. In this book, he is called Erland and is currently 21 years old. Erland was quite abandoned when he came here. His gaze was quite bland and the whole was perceived as being given up. Quite soon, I would keep this under my protective wings, not because I know why I felt so, just for the moment. It was more natural to protect the kid, so he did not find anything negative. He had not been on the prison before. Everyone who has sat on the prison knows that things can quickly change into a sharp position, because of a word. The kid could not, the language used on the prison. So that was a challenge for me. Erland took over my work as the department's cleaner. Because I had stroke, some points became difficult because I have very bad balance. So Erland took over my job. Erland was kind and helped me with the information I had, even though he was a bit tired of tomorrow, so he went along. In a couple of weeks, I talked to Erland about his future. There is no doubt that Erland is bad about all the negative things he has done. His family has involuntarily been a part of Erland's commitments. Erland has in a very negative way put his criminal things into effect without taking responsibility for the consequences that hit him, but not least his family. His mother, dad, siblings and others have probably not claimed Erland.

Erland has used one-way duplex. This has meant that Erland has been able to execute certain points. Probably the family has not claimed any claims, because they did not want a conflict. Erland has succeeded in doing things... But Erland really succeeded? Yes! It certainly wondered the defenders as well. Erland is a good guy who has proven to have consequences for the crimes he has performed. Just that he's doing right in the future, it's just him who can control it. I think he succeeded, and his family is worth not to feel the worries that Erland succeeded in developing. The cost of Erland's prominent ways has been a mental and great expense for his family. His biological father even drove out liquid funds after Erland asked for money. I understand why his dad has acted like that. Since he probably does not want a conflict with Erland, who may not belong to the father hereafter. Erland has used their parents as they live in different directions. However, in the same town.

Erland has played the strings that the situation required, in order to achieve and achieve the goal that Erland wants. Everything else was totally uninteresting for Erland. When Erland's mother gave him money, Erland would not buy some things for these liquid funds. Erland thought it was disrespectful to her mother. When his biological father brought money to Erland, Erland did not consider it a problem to buy some things for this money. Erland has values, but I find no logical explanation. Erland probably has its own list that symbolizes important things for him personally. So I think it's ... Erland has many good qualities that he should use in the future.

Chapter 56: Robin

Want to tell you about a man I met on my prison. His name is Robin. Since 1995, Robin has been an ordinary person who had lived in accordance with the laws in our society. Would like to describe him for those who read these lines so you can get a picture of what he looks like. Robin is a middle aged man who could go at his own pace through life. There is probably nothing that hurts him. In any case, not to sit on duty. He is very calm as a person, I do not get directly bothered by him, I think he is a very good person. In writing, I have walked twice with him. Two Saturdays, Robin and I have taken a walk. He has been sentenced to ten years in Swedish court and has influenced him and his family a lot. What he is convicted of, I will tell you later. But right now, I want you to hear what consequences Robin and his family have suffered, this verdict that has proven to affect Robin's entire family. As I said earlier, Robin has been an ordinary person who has provided his family with his income. Robin has always been an entrepreneur who has made his way.

Robin has always been able to support, his family in the above manner. Robin has lived a quiet and tidy life. However, with modification, at least a quiet life. I'm very hard to see him a criminal who had ten years on this prison. The society and the correctional do not like that.

But what is he then convicted of? Yes, for serious drug offenses. When the Court of Appeal said, the sentence was ten years. Robin then chose that to talk to his family and not least with his wife. Robin told his wife that she could go on and that he would not do anything about it. His wife replied that she wanted to wait for him and that they are married yet and have children together. Robin is a good person who deserves his punishment. So I really hope he gets a job that he really deserves. Not least his wife, who has been waiting for him all the time forever.

I want to talk about a person called Harald. Harald handled the carpentry where I practiced a couple of times a week. I got to practice my fine engine. I did not understand then that it was a good person. He did not say much from the beginning, but it became more and more. Finally, we learned to feel each other a bit better, or quite well. Harald, he was grossly economical, that was what symbolized him for the most part. Anyway, so he trained me when I went, he trained me when I was going to learn to go at all, taught me to walk on uneven surfaces. He taught me to get up on a hill which a commonperson likes to be pissed off easily, but when you've had a stroke it's not that easy. He was a pretty important person to me, he is, of course, now also, and even more under my stroke, and he never let go. He made sure that it went ahead for me although I did not think it was so great fun. I went to the gymnastics gym and practiced my fine engine there. There was someone I called the Grayleg, he had gray hair and was usually dressed in gray and gray in hair and clothes, so you get pretty gray. It was only the soul that was a little brighter. Anyway, he was called Grayleg. Those two, Harald and Grayleg were those had to practice this I for who symbolized my new life now after the stroke. Today it was hand gymnastics and for those who do not know what it is, you sit at a table and do different exercises. You stretch your shoulders, neck, hands, and then try to put your hand and, fingers together in a special way. Again, it sounds pissed off easily, but when the signals between the brain and the fingers do not go so well, it's not that easy. a long time. I had no power in either right or left hand. I had to measure my strength and translated into Swedish so I was about so strong that you could almost lift a liter of milk. No, I can not say it was so funny. I was quite tired of those exercises. You should measure your strength as I said, and I did not have one of our patients, and then I became cursed to be braintired. They had a restroom in the infirmary where we had to go to bed and we would be too tired. After 5 - 10 minutes of such exercises, you had to sleep, or I had to sleep. You lay down and sleep, and you really did, I slept very much. In the same restroom, sister Marie, a happy person, she took the blood pressure on me, preferably when I had rested, as was done quite often. However, sister Marie took my blood pressure 3 times a week for my doctor to have a complete overview of my health. I can say afterwards that had not been for Harald's training when you learned to go, Grayleg's hand gymnastics and when you reach your neck and shoulders and sister Maries check my blood pressure, I honestly believe that I had not been so good shape that I am today. Today I can almost run out, yes, maybe it was a bit overpowering, but it can go quite fast. I can move both right and left without any problems. I can say that during the training I had, none of the above people were so popular and their shares were not high. That rate was quite low, I have to say that. The carpenter Harald was a very special person. Normally, you would want to hit the nail with your right hand, but now I was better with your left hand. So it meant that now I would train my right hand and knock, down the nail. It was not that great fun because sometimes you met the nail, but usually not. So it was pretty much easier to change your hand and knock, down the nail to the left. Harald tried to train most of what just went, and he was almost happy every day, I almost said-He was never satisfied. One day Harald said he had talked to my doctor and he said we would go to make some food and then eat the food, and for me it was, hmm, do some food.

You would then try to cook in a small kitchen in the hospital if you could, how to handle some things in the kitchen, for example, knives, forks, pouring up if you could insert a key in the door lock. But no matter what it was, Harald had a terrible patience, I did not myself and I can not say I have nu either. No matter what, he stands there, minute after minute, and I'm just more annoyed by myself, but Harald stays and he is, as stubborn and calm. No, he will not be stressed, I can say. Today, I'm very happy I met Harald, he means very much to me, even though he is a very special person.

The Grayleg was also one of those people I thought was important to me. He coached me more in balance. We could play bowling on a TV game just because I'd learn to keep the balance, now it sounds terribly simple, it was just not. I have never felt so drunk and yet so sober at the same time. Just lifting a leg was an art called Duga. But even there, Grayleg was very patient, he decided to help me in the best way, and he did. With success, apparently. So, I can only say thank you to you, Grayleg, thank you so much for all your help.

To sister Marie, I also want to say thank you. We had our

talk time about both the one and the other. You chose to make sure I could handle myself and I have done so you know. Anyway, I would just like to say so much to you for all your help.

Yes, and then it was Harald. The man, the myth, the legend, he is economical. Anyway, to you I would like to say thank you. I know supervisor I would also like to say thank you for arranging my furniture and making sure it worked when we played both bowling, chess, and everything just went on one thing, that I would get better. That I could handle certain situations and I do today. So I just want to say thank you to Harald, thank you for all your help. Hope to hear from you soon.

To Mom G.M. I've got a mother that has adopted me and it feels very good, where she has managed to deal with my bad mood from the prison (Institution), which probably was not so easy when I was annoyed and angry on a guard and where you always kept your inner calm, how it's going on now. I have always felt that you are by my side, and it feels safe, even though you sometimes wonder how your son is and if he's still calm. Understand it is, not easy with a son who has other values. Mom you can be calm ... your son has calmed down and is, not going to sit on the prison anymore.

To Pelle janitor ... Yes, what should I say to this ETERNAL DARKNESS! No Pelle, I'm just kidding with you. You were my supervisor on the prisontime and you would learn me a lot of things. Pelle it went very well, but forgot to say something. Now I understood quite quickly that you did not like talking all the time, but maybe it was fun if you said more than three words a week. To me you are a very good person ... which is QUIET ALL THE TIME that I like. Would like to thank you and PO for any help.

The other employees I want to say that I am very grateful for all the help and, support you gave me while I was on the prison.

It was time for me to be released from prison. It was finally time. I know I did not sleep the night before. I started packing everything that was in my closet, and I had pulled a lot of them all, so it got a lot of packing. I had to buy a bag of the correctional so that I could accommodate everything. Anyway, that night before I'm going to be released, I honestly think I did not sleep for a second. I probably was expecting how society would receive me when I came out after serving my punishment. I did not immediately have a home when I came out. However, my deputy supervisor Karlsson had arranged so that I had both a internship and an apartment when I had been released.

In the morning at 7:00 pm I went to the Central Guard, I would be released after all these years on the prison. It was my turn and it felt damn good. The guards knew me, as I have said, they have lived for a long time so it is clear they felt quite well. I also think they were a little nervous how Persson would be when he got into society. On the other side, that is, the Smithworld, my deputy supervisor Karlsson had done a huge job. She had both arranged an internship for me and a home I would live in which was quite big can be said. When I left the prison, it felt a bit strange indeed. I left there in my own clothes, I had no guards after me, I was not wanted, I had to be out for more than 72 hours. So yes it felt strangely strange. I knew I would meet my deputy supervisor Karlsson soon and I would get my home where I was going to live. She herself had seen it, I did not know what it looked like or what was there or something at all. I only knew that I trusted my vice supervisor. I could not imagine she would put me in a difficult situation. Evidently, she did not, I got a very nice residence where I got a separate contract. I would pay rent, and be a regular Smith in a society that would have a former villain. How this would happen, or how the effect of this would be.

I came to my new home, we met, me and my deputy supervisor, by the landlord, and we walked around and looked at the apartment. I thought it was very nice. Now the landlord wanted to sign a contract and all I had written was my permission, and my released. I did not write anything else, so it was unbelievably strange to sit and sign my own contract from the prospective landlord. It is probably quite difficult to get into that situation, but it was very strange, I can promise you. The landlord went away, my deputy supervisor Karlsson stayed for a while, and after she went. Where did I stand? Not a guard as far the eye reached, not anyone. I could do just what I wanted, but it's badly strange that you do not. Because I do not think you've landed purely mentally when I go through this procedure. I did not want to go out, everyone else who had now been released would go out but not me. I just wanted to be inside my apartment. Ideally, I wanted to be in the shithouse because it was as big as my cell. Stranges you are like a person. But I tried to adapt to them in the next few days in a more positive way and, as soon as someone saw the window, one went from there. It was quite ordinary people, it was a very foamy feeling. The bags I had with me from the prison had just packed up the most important watch. The rest was left in the bags. I sat down on a chair and wondered what the hell this would be like. I knew I would, not to start my internship until 3 days. But in my terms it means 72 hours, it was like a permission. Imagine going to an internship. Quite strange. I could not think of them the courses. I could not help myself to go to work and have coworkers. Yes, for me it was totally unbelievable. It was almost that you would pinch your arm and wake up from this dream, because this was just too much. I know when it became Sunday night, I became in some form of paralyzed, I knew I would go to my internship at 7:00 AM on Monday morning. Nevertheless, I doubted that this would happen. If I was injured so that I could not understand it myself. I know I was watching TV, it felt like sitting on the prison, I was sitting myself, I was just waiting for someone to lock the celldoor again, and say good night. Nobody came, there was no one who said goodnight. The question was just who the hell is going to unlock the door when I going to the shithouse, nobody was here, or I will not lock. Yes, a little exaggerated, but you definitely understand what I mean. I was so upset and, institution injured that the guards would do everything to one. Because when you sit on the prison, you do not have to think, it makes the authority one. Monday morning came and I would go to my internship. I had to meet the boss and already a very strange feeling was revealed, he was as happy and calm as everyone else, except myself. I had to meet my future colleagues, then he was doing some work. Because I had a stroke, there was some kind of job training, because they did not know what capacity I had. I worked from

07:00 to 11:00, then I went home. I was terribly tired. I was home at 11:30 to 12:00 and then I slept for about 12 hours. I was completely over. Probably it was the all new, impressions I have received and all new people who were actually nice and kind. Everyone thought it was fun, that there had been a new, person there. Everyone except me. I just thought it was uncomfortable, it felt uncontrollable to me who came straight from the prison and had ben released 3 days ago. So there were actually some mixed, feelings then it was day in and day out. I had to go out with the manager sometimes, who was in the service industry. It caused me to fall asleep in the car, I was so tired that it can not be imagined. The boss, or "SB" as his name and his wife "AB", invited me a few times to food so I could get down to earth and meet quite ordinary people. Which I did. I got there and met his wife, felt strange too. I could not easily adapt to the situation that had been discovered. I did not know why. Probably I had not landed and I was not really there mentally yet. However, the dinner went well, after that some coffee was taken and then running my boss me home. I know I did not say that much that night. I did not have much to say, I had more thoughts than words. When I got home, I just thanked for the ride, and went into my apartment and tried to calm down myself. Inside me it felt strange. It felt like I was as shaky as an aspen leaf, but it did not seem beyond me. I try to adapt myself to this new, situation as per day. The boss "SB" and I had quite a few discussions, but not the first time, but then I started to get more adapted and asked some questions about how it works out in society, which I once was a part of. The boss "SB" said it was good as it always seems to be, so there was no big difference for his part. That was it for me. Because I was part of this society, I was not there anymore. I certainly had earned my punishment, but had society accepted it or not. As you understand, there were quite a few questions and I can not say that the answers are loose with their presence right away. I tried to stick with my boss "SB" so long as it went.

There was certainly another person who in this book is called "Johan the stingy man". Have also met his wife "BR", and it was nice people there too. They were very nice people. Johan, who was a little bit stingy, so I called him "Johan the stingy man", yes, you have to choose what you want, but he was good at all. He tried to get me on the right side of the law in an easy way. Now it was not straightforward either to me or to Johan. It was the situation that occurred there, "Johan the stingy man" would solve the situation in his way, and I with my baseball tree, now we did not really agree on this so it created more discussions than success to start with. I had my values from the prison, and only now I noticed that when I got into society, people had totally different values, so it actually became problematic. According to society, one could not solve the situation with a baseball tree or with violence as they did on the prison. Johan was not so easy to talk, you can not say that right away. He was the way he was, he is the way he is. You can not do that much. I think and I really hope that my part will be better with my values. I can not say in writing it's better or worse. I think more that I am neutral and try to survive in the present moment in a healthy and sensible manner. But again, it's just about a thing, values. It is absolutely nothing but values. Johan and his wife "BR" also invited me to dinner a number of times, and probably tried to make me adapt to this society that I do not belong to today. I'm really trying, but it feels more like breaking the elbow in the wrong direction, it goes but it hurts badly. I hope my discussions with "Johan the stingy man" and the boss "SB" and their wives will give me something in the future so I can adapt. Because I want to mentally adapt, right now I feel like I just can not, just can not. I think too much crime, while I hate crime. I think violence, but I do not like violence, and I can disturb it. For that reason, I suddenly have begun to tame my own values and try to adapt to one, as I say, a corrupt society. But as it is now, I really hope that it has gone a little further. We will see what the future has to offer. It will turn out, I'm totally convinced.

I would also like to talk about a woman called "Ulrika Frustration". It is a woman I have difficulty describing, she has some other values. Do not ask me which, because I do not know, probably do not even know scientists this. At least, it's not my values. Why I choose to pick up "Ulrika Frustration" is because, for the first time in my life, I realize that someone has influenced me, and strongly. Whether it's positive or negative, or if it's for me to adapt, in this society or not. I really do not know. I only know that right now, I am very doubtful and honestly, I do not know at the time of writing, neither on nor behind in this question that proves to affect my life. It's a woman who has amazing qualities and she's incredibly intelligent, yet gives this person a brand, new face for the FRUSTRATION. I really hope that this frustration brings with you, and all these questions get an answer that all parties can accept in the future.

I am now in a society in which I will be involved, and for which I should be involved. Where society must, accept me as a citizen. Nevertheless, it feels like you know, the feeling of the cream on the coffee, you float a little on top. That's why this book is called "In the Shadow of Society" because that's just how it feels. I know today that I have good people around me all the time. The boss "SB", his wife "AB", "Johan the stingy man" and his wife "BR" are great, yet I can not, at the moment, adapt me. I try to take care of the law, pay my bills. But it still feels like you do not do these things, why should I do it then? Society demands that you do it. Nevertheless, society demands another to take care, but I do not feel that I am accepted in society. Even though I deserved my punishment, I have taken my punishment, so why can not society accept me. I have not violated the law, I have done my, I have done many illegal things, but I have earned my punishment. I am absolutely convinced that anyone who should have a penalty has not taken his punishment. I probably know that I will not write more memos or autobiographies throughout my life. I now feel that I'm done with my trip. There have been 4 books, so I feel like I've been writing. I have got to know the words in full, I have seen the corrupt society, as I will become a Smith in. There people say one thing, but mean another. In the criminal world, it does not work, and it knows all who have been there, but not so many. There are about 5,000 people a year, but no matter what, I'm absolutely convinced that I will do my utmost to become an ordinary Smith.

Finally!

I want to watch and thank all the people who read my books, and have taken the time to get into my situation, which certainly affected many people. It has been a long journey where I as a person have changed in the meantime. Unfortunately, I've been involved in many illegal things, and have been severely beaten by myself. I've been with very sick people who have done gross crimes. I have seen both the Action Strength and the black group on the prison (Institution) where we Inmates really hated these guards, and violence is the solution of both sides to the problem. Once upon a time, just a regular person, and during the journey, has become a full-fledged villain. A villain that was chased by KUT, chased by Interpol, where I was internationally requested. The criminal intelligence service for a few years later. Then it's not that easy to be able to adapt to society, when I've been 20 years old in the so-called cold. Just hope society can accept me now, and in the future.

Thanks for the word.
The author
Jesper Persson